He was the serpent in her Eden—the ultimate temptation.

"Miss Wellsley—the missionary?" he asked incredulously.

"Yes, I'm Cassandra Wellsley."

From the trail, his hair had appeared blond. Now she could see that it was iron gray, with a spattering of black. Adam Ralston's youthful face belied his age though he couldn't be much past forty—young for his responsible position with Pacific Lumber.

"Let's get right to the point, Miss Wellsley. I didn't trek through miles of jungle this morning for a social call. I'm here to talk business."

"Nor would we be likely to invite you for a social call, Mr. Ralston," she retorted.

A stony silence prevailed as Cassandra considered his errand. Unless Adam Ralston could be persuaded to plead their cause before the officials of his company, theirs would be the next valley to be logged, destroying years of painstaking work with the tribe.

"I must admit you aren't exactly what I expected to find when I set out this morning." The man surveyed her lazily, speculatively. "I think George Sanders left out a lot when he convinced me to visit the compound before making my final recommendation. Does he know what an explosive powder keg you are?"

"Only when there is someone around to light the fuse."

"Touché! I guess that makes us even, Miss Wellsley. I wonder how long we'll keep that score."

FOREVER EDEN

Barbara Bennett

Serenade/Serenata
BOOKS
of the Zondervan Publishing House
Grand Rapids, Michigan

FOREVER EDEN
Copyright © 1985 by Barbara Bennett
Serenade Serenata is an imprint of
The Zondervan Publishing House
1415 Lake Drive, S.E.
Grand Rapids, Michigan 49506

ISBN 0-310-46712-8

Edited by Anne Severance
Designed by Kim Koning

Printed in the United States of America

85 86 87 88 89 90 / 10 9 8 7 6 5 4 3 2

To my husband Paul
and daughters, Amy and Allison.
May we grow closer to one another
as we grow closer to the Lord.

ACKNOWLEDGMENTS

A special thanks to furloughed Philippine missionaries, Bryan and Diane Thomas. The Thomases' insight into both the work and the people of the Philippines added a dimension of understanding to this story that could not have been realized without them.

Thank you, Bryan and Diane, for your assistance with FOREVER EDEN, and more importantly, for the friendship we've shared these past twelve years.

CHAPTER 1

CASSANDRA WELLSLEY KNEW she was beautiful—and she hated it! Dark honeyed hair fell in gentle curls about her face, kissing softly the smooth bronzed skin beneath it. Thickly fringed eyes of deep blue stared back at her from the mirrored reflection. They narrowed as Cassandra viewed what to her had more often seemed a thorn in the flesh than a blessing. A half-smile passed delicately defined lips as she thought of all those who envied her in their ignorance.

With a sigh of resignation she turned from the offending glass, prepared to start another day. No one here cared about her looks; the value system was different, though, in its own way just as false as any other. But for Cassandra, her jungle home was a little slice of Eden—where she belonged, where God wanted her to be.

Nestled among the waxy leaves of a small banana grove, her cottage looked out on a lush garden. The brightly colored bougainvillaea Cassandra had transplanted during her first year in Mindanao now trailed effortlessly along the length of the small front porch. Wild orchids sprang up in abandon, like exquisite ballerinas taking a bow, their graceful lines adding a certain sophistication to the untamed setting. The morning sun rose above the towering trees, casting fleeting shadows on the village.

It felt muggy despite the cooling tropical breeze that blew through the open door. Though she had been born in a northern state, most of Cassandra's twenty-seven years had been spent little more than a stone's throw from the site where the winding waters of the Mississippi River and the great Gulf shake hands. Adjusting to the humid climate of the Philippines had required minimum effort for her, but she often wondered about her teammate. Jodi Campbell was from Montana. Growing up only ten miles from the Canadian border, Jodi had barely known the meaning of the word *summer* before accepting the post in Mindanao. Here it was always summer, and always hot.

Venturing outside and descending the porch's half-dozen steps, Cassandra spotted the petite brunette near the edge of the small clearing. Jodi was talking with Fely, one of the tribal women. A gnarled old coconut palm formed a perfect seat for the two of them, its trunk bending so low in one place it almost touched the ground.

"Good morning," Cassandra greeted them, trying to ignore the anxious looks on both faces.

"Morning," Jodi returned, Fely briefly flashing her broad, partially toothless smile.

The older woman's two sons were up the hill, watching for the arrival of their guests. But the majority of the tribe seemed unaware of the significance of this day, going about their business as usual. Cassandra watched silently as the men headed out to tend their crops, to hunt or fish. The women, with babies strapped to their backs, were pounding rice, or taking the family wash down to the river to beat upon the rocks until clean. These were a people frozen in time, quietly going about their tasks as their parents and grandparents before them. But she loved them and couldn't view them as did many others—primitive savages whose half-clad bodies frequently peopled the glossy pages of some anthropological magazine. The inhabitants of this small valley were her friends—her family—and she had no intention of giving up everything they'd worked for without a fight!

"The regional project manager for the Pacific Lumber Company, along with his band of merry men, has been seen on the trail," Jodi stated sarcastically. "Adam Ralston. With a name like Adam, you might say he's come to reclaim Eden." There was no levity in her voice. "But the way I see it, he's more like the serpent."

"How long ago?" Cassandra asked practically, choosing to censure her usually easygoing companion with only a look. Jodi's feelings, however, weren't far from her own. "Did Bobbit say?" Cassandra asked his mother.

"Twenty, thirty minutes," Fely declared in her own tongue, relaying the message her son had given. Her eyes were hopeful as she smiled up at Cassandra. "*Day* will make it right, no?"

"I'll try," Cassandra promised, marveling that she could still be called "young woman." She felt as if the events of the past week had aged her noticeably.

Despite official protests the mission's appeal to the logging company had been denied. Those eager to cash in on the island's lucrative lumber supply were more concerned with profit than with the eternal well-being of the natives, she thought bitterly. Cassandra just had to convince Adam Ralston to listen to reason.

If the villagers were dispersed now to make way for the felling of trees, much of what she had labored to accomplish in the last three years would be lost. They had to have more time.

"Pray . . ." muttered Cassandra. "Pray I don't put my foot in it!"

"What?" Fely's puzzled expression told her something had been lost in the translation.

"Never mind," Cassandra laughed, not bothering to explain. "Just pray!"

With a shrug of her tiny shoulders Fely headed in the direction of her own hut, where the handful of believers was already gathering. It was not yet a church; but, given time, it would be. They had traveled a slow road, but thankfully until now, at least, a steady one.

Jumping down suddenly from her perch, Jodi's brown eyes flashed, as if reality had just dawned. "You're not ready!" she exclaimed. "You can't wear that thing!"

"Why not?" Defensively Cassandra eyed the green and yellow print of the shapeless one-piece skirt she had neatly tied above her breasts. "I always wear a *mahlong* around here. You have one on."

"Well . . . yes," Jodi admitted, glancing down, unimpressed. "But I'm short and skinny . . . not tall and gorgeous. Mine covers up what no one wants to see, but yours . . ."

"He's coming to see me as a missionary—not as a woman."

"And they've already turned down the missionaries."

A stony silence prevailed as Cassandra considered her friend's words. It was true—official channels had gotten nowhere with Pacific Lumber. Unless Adam Ralston advised differently, theirs would be the next valley to be logged. The mission needed him on their

10

side, but Cassandra preferred that the project manager's support be prompted by belief in their purpose, not by the beauty of the missionary in charge.

"You could wear the blue sundress your Uncle Geo sent you," Jodi urged, her eyes wide and hopeful. "And maybe a touch of make-up?"

Cassandra hated to disappoint Jodi, but the lovely birthday present would have to debut another day. "No dress . . . no make-up," she stated emphatically. "I'll wash up and run a brush through my hair, but no more."

Jodi eyed the shapeless *mahlong* with disgust. "It's a good thing you've got such a pretty face, because without it you'd never catch anyone's attention wearing that thing!"

"Oh, I don't know, . . ." Cassandra teased, her smile easing the growing tension. "If it was attention I wanted, I could always wear my *mahlong* around my waist like most of the native women."

"You've got a point," Jodi admitted with a chuckle. "But I wasn't suggesting anything quite so drastic." Turning with Cassandra toward the house, she walked the short distance to the steps. "Does headquarters know about this side of your nature? Maybe next time George calls, I should talk to him about your absorbing *too* much culture."

"Do that over the air, and they'll be taking our radio away from us!" Laughing, Cassandra raced up the steps, beating Jodi through the door.

As Cassandra walked past the radio, she wished for the thousandth time she could hear from George. Uncle Geo, as she fondly referred to him, wasn't really her uncle—more like a distant cousin by marriage. Nevertheless, he was a dear friend who knew her better than she knew herself, and she could use some encouragement right now. Today, however, he wouldn't be making the daily radio contacts from Butuan. And next week, when he returned from Manila, would be too late. In a few minutes she would have to confront Adam Ralston—alone.

This waiting game was getting on her nerves, and she paced the floor of the small living room restlessly. The worn cotton material of the *mahlong* played around her calves, its faded print contrasting with delicate, but vibrant features. Eyes as blue as any ocean peered past the window and out into the lush vegetation.

"I think I see them." Her calm voice belied the nervousness she felt. Much was riding on the success of this encounter with the representative of the logging company.

"Where?" Rushing to the window, Jodi strained for a glimpse of the four figures walking down the tree-lined path, but without her glasses she could make out little. "Which one do you think is Adam?"

"If he's the one in the loincloth, *you're* the one who's overdressed!"

"You're no help!" Grabbing her case off the counter, Jodi decided to see for herself. "That's Fely's youngest," she sighed. "You knew that! Adam Ralston must be the tall man in the middle. The other two are Filipinos." Watching Jodi surreptitiously replace her glasses in the case, Cassandra smiled at her friend's reluctance to wear the recently prescribed lenses. "What do you think they're here for?"

"The Filipinos?" The kettle whistled from the stove and Cassandra walked over and turned off the flame. "He probably brought them to map the area." The heels of her sandals clicked on the wooden floor as Cassandra removed the kettle and poured the boiling water into a ceramic teapot. "Do we have any more of those tinned cookies?" Serving light refresh-

12

ments was always an icebreaker in awkward situations. "Never mind. I found them."

Jodi's full attention was still focused on the group now only fifty yards or so from the clearing. "They're almost here!" she shouted, causing Cassandra to break one of the butter cookies she was arranging on a plate. "How do I look?" Jodi's crumpled *mahlong* had been discarded for a pretty yellow jumpsuit.

"Good enough to eat." Cassandra smiled at her young friend, happy for once she wasn't berating herself. Jodi's features were too plain to be called attractive, but by most accounts were pleasant enough.

A firm knock sounded at the door, and Cassandra dropped the loaded tray with a thud onto the weathered old coffee table. Cheap china cups rattled in angry protest, and Cassandra's gaze froze upon the brightly colored cushions of the wicker couch. It was ridiculous to be so nervous, she knew, yet much depended on these next few moments.

Jodi opened the door. "Miss Wellsley?" Cassandra turned at the sound of the clearly masculine voice.

"No . . ."

" *I'm* Cassandra Wellsley."

Adam Ralston's frankly admiring gaze had a hypnotic effect on Cassandra. His pale blue eyes drank in every inch of her until his expression suddenly snapped shut, like a steel trap, closing out all emotion. "I'm Adam Ralston, from Pacific Lumber." His tone was decidedly cold and formal.

"Yes . . . I know," she faltered, wondering if she had only imagined the initial warmth. "We've been expecting you."

From a distance his hair had appeared blond, but Cassandra could now see it was iron gray with a spattering of black. Adam Ralston's youthful face belied his age, though he couldn't be much over forty.

13

He was as impressive a man as Cassandra had ever met.

Dark, full brows almost met over an aquiline nose as he surveyed the room. His eyes narrowed when he saw the tea tray. "What have we here?" Ralston's tone was condescending, making Cassandra feel uncomfortable, even gauche.

"We thought you might like something after your long walk." The man was infuriating! Cassandra's patience was already wearing thin. "I'm afraid this is the best we can offer. The neighborhood store was out of fresh *croissants*, and even our coffee ration was misrouted this month."

Tension hung in the air like dark snow clouds on a December morning. His jaw flexing, Adam Ralston stepped into the room. Picking up one of the cookies, he eyed it distastefully. "Let's get right to the point, Miss Wellsley. I didn't trek through miles of jungle this morning for a tea party. I came to talk business."

"Good . . ." Cassandra smiled, her eyes as cold as his own, ". . . because I doubt we would ever care to invite you socially, Mr. Ralston." Ignoring her partner's pale face and warning look, Cassandra defiantly poured Jodi and herself a cup of tea. Placing two cookies on a plate, she leisurely walked around the table and took a seat on the couch. "Would you care to sit down, Mr. Ralston?" Freeing a hand, she indicated the chair to her far right. "Or would you prefer to continue standing over us, playing lord and master?"

Puzzled by the fleeting smile she saw cross his face, Cassandra and Jodi watched as he accepted her grudging invitation. "Where'd they find *you*?" he asked with an unexpected laugh.

Jodi and Cassandra exchanged glances, not knowing if they should be relieved or frightened.

"I'm not crazy," he assured them, still chuckling.

"But let's face it, Miss Cassandra Wellsley, you aren't exactly what I expected to find when I set out this morning." Leaning back in the chair, Adam Ralston folded his arms, surveying her lazily, speculatively. "No . . . George Sanders sure left out a lot when he convinced me to visit the compound before making my final recommendation. Does he know what an explosive powder keg you are?"

"Only when there is someone around to light the fuse."

"Touché!" he laughed. "I was rude." His admission was no less than truth. "It was just . . . well, it doesn't matter."

Cassandra's eyes narrowed this time, certain that it mattered very much. Her intuition told her it was important to know the cause of Adam Ralston's almost instant resentment.

Avoiding her scrutiny, he shifted to Jodi, giving her a broad smile. "You must be Miss Campbell." Accepting her nod, he reached into his back pocket and took out a sheet of folded notepaper. "According to George, you're the linguist."

"Yes, I guess you could say so," Jodi acknowledged. "Cassandra also helps with the language and culture files. I compile the data." Nervously she glanced at her friend, hoping she'd take over. "My strengths lie with words, but Cassandra is much better with the people."

"Really?"

"*Most* people, that is!" Cassandra countered.

"Just not arrogant lumber managers?"

They shared a smile that was a kind of truce, but it didn't keep her from speculating about this enigma of a man. Usually she was able to keep a tight rein on her annoying temper, but evidently not where Adam Ralston was concerned. He intrigued her more than

15

she cared to admit. It wasn't often a man received, let alone held, her attention.

Cassandra watched as he spoke, following the lean line of his jaw. Even, white teeth flashed from behind thinned lips that shaped questions about the progress of their work. Jodi's answers became increasingly animated, Cassandra noticed, in direct proportion to Adam Ralston's display of charm. She smiled at the thought of her partner's earlier description of this engaging intruder—the serpent in Eden. Given time, he might have naïve Jodi Campbell eating out of his hand, but Cassandra Wellsley wasn't at all certain she trusted him—nor was she sure she wanted to.

Absently she pushed an errant curl behind her ear, thinking of how Adam Ralston compared to other men she'd met. Ruggedly attractive, he reminded her of the stern-looking models in the fashion magazines her Aunt Ernestine still insisted upon sending her. Pretty-boy faces and sun-bleached blonds were no longer the rage, as when she'd spent hours under the hot photography lights. That one-year contract with Randolph Martin had seemed an eternity then, but now it was hard to believe she had ever glittered in that tinsel world. Even at eighteen it hadn't taken long for the excitement to wear off. Cassandra often wondered when she came across a familiar face, with body draped in the latest fashion, whether her former friend still found the profession rewarding. She'd learned quickly that the lifestyle was too plastic an existence for her, too shallow for one's life's goal.

Shock waves had rocked the agency when Cassandra refused to renew her contract. Her parents had been supportive of her decision, not because they fully understood, but because they believed their children should be free to choose their own paths. Mitch and Michael, her seventeen-year-old twin

16

brothers, didn't care; their lives revolved around football and girls.

But Cassandra's Aunt Ernestine was furious! Dropping everything, she'd boarded a plane from Philadelphia the very day she'd heard the news. When she arrived at her brother's house, she left no doubt as to the source of Cassandra's own bothersome temper. Aunt Ernestine had been pacing the floor when her niece entered the room.

"Missions!" she'd bellowed, undeterred by Cassandra's determined stance. "I thought we'd cleared that nonsense out of your head last year." Her green eyes narrowed like a cat studying her prey. "I have plans for you, my dear—big plans."

The scene replayed in Cassandra's mind like a videotape, recalling the events of the night almost eight years ago. Her parents were not home, having already left for a local church to hear Millie and George Sanders's presentation of their mission work. The Sanderses had been on emergency furlough due to Millie's health but, with her recovery, they would soon be returning to the field. Cassandra had hoped for a shower and change before joining them, but with her aunt's sudden visit, these plans were altered.

Now she knew it had been silly to think Ernestine Powers would not know about her decision to leave the modeling field. Her aunt's grapevine had probably delivered the information within minutes of her leaving Mr. Martin's office. Judging by his reaction, Cassandra felt certain the leak had been Randolph Martin himself. There had been no phone at the location session, and the reshooting of a whole page of the layout had thrown Cassandra's schedule way off. She had planned to call after the meeting, but her aunt had made it unnecessary.

"I was afraid of something like this when I heard that your mother's cousin and that meddling husband

17

of hers were in town." It had taken every ounce of patience Cassandra possessed not to come to the Sanderses' defense. She'd watched as her aunt paced nervously. Not a hair of her head dared to leave its place; like the black wings of a raven, it gleamed. "I could strangle those two for messing with your mind! If they want to throw away their lives in some stupid jungle, then let them."

"I'm not throwing away my life," she stated calmly, unable to stay silent.

"No?" Her aunt's laugh had been almost hysterical. "Do you really believe those natives care any more about their souls than . . . than *I* do?" Cassandra remembered the finely chiseled features of the ex-model tightening at her own words, and her well-manicured hand fingering a button on her expensive silk blouse. "I'm doing quite well, thank you. I don't need your God, Cassandra, and neither do they."

It wasn't the first time she had heard her aunt use such words. Cassandra's failure to reach those closest to her for the Lord had been discouraging, but she realized even then her job was not to convert, but to remain faithful. The decision to trust Christ as Savior lay with the individual and God, but the work of telling rested with the Christian. Even in the tribe she could only inform, share, persuade, and live a consistent life before them—she couldn't *make* them believe.

CHAPTER 2

THOUGHTS OF THE TRIBE jarred Cassandra abruptly back to the present. Two puzzled faces stared at her bemused expression.

"I'm sorry," she mumbled, still caught up in her reverie. "I . . . I don't usually do that. I'm afraid I'm the one who has been rude this time."

Adam Ralston raked a broad hand through his hair as he rose impatiently from the couch. "I guess that makes us even, Miss Wellsley." Well over six feet, he towered above her, but his crooked smile cast him more in the role of a gentle giant. Gone, for the moment at least, was the menacing enemy who had touched off her anger. "I wonder how long we'll keep that score?"

"Fifteen-fifteen, Mr. Ralston?"

"Adam." The fine lines around his eyes crinkled as his grin widened. "Only my closest friends call me Mr. Ralston."

Cassandra noticed the slightest of dimples as she

accepted his outstretched hand and was helped to her feet. "Where are we going?"

"The clinic," Jodi supplied, "didn't you hear us?"

"No, I'm afraid I didn't." The admission embarrassed her, but it was the truth. "Mr. Ralston—"

"Adam," he corrected, humor dancing in his eyes. "No liberties allowed, Miss Wellsley."

"None intended . . ." narrowing eyes censored her words, ". . . Adam." A resigned sigh and a sudden smile followed her capitulation. "I guess that means you should call me Cassandra."

Jodi lifted the tray and headed for the kitchen. "You could live dangerously and call her Cassie," she suggested over her shoulder mischievously. "But there is only one person I know who has done it and lived to tell about it."

Evidently the two of them had struck up quite a friendship during their conversation. Jodi seemed at ease with Adam Ralston, causing Cassandra to wonder what they had talked about. If she hadn't been daydreaming, she'd know. Either she had misjudged him, or Jodi was slipping. Even in this more congenial mood, however, she felt strangely threatened by Adam Ralston, and she knew it had little to do with his having the power to move the tribe and cripple their work. She was afraid to get along with him, afraid of where things might lead if she actually began to like him.

Adam's presence filled the room. He was so close Cassandra could study the stylish cut of his gray hair and the subtle shadings of blue in his eyes, as he studied *her*. Humor danced in their moist haven, captivating her as he spoke. "He must be some fellow to get away with that." Lazily he lifted her chin with his left hand, his stare daring her to remove it. "Was he the one you were so lost in thought about?"

It took a moment for the meaning to register.

Schoolgirls, not grown women, wasted their time mooning over men, Cassandra reasoned smugly. "I think you have the wrong idea, Mr. Ralston." Somehow, she was unable to call him "Adam."

"I hope so," he stated, releasing her chin. "Any man tame enough to sit home and patiently wait for you to come out of the jungle wouldn't be man enough to keep you—Cassie."

The challenge was there. She wished she could wipe his crooked smile from his face. His advice was unwanted and the use of her nickname too intimate. Until that moment she hadn't noticed the gold band on his third finger, left hand. "Does your wife sit home and patiently wait for you to come out of the jungle?" she smiled tightly.

"She might . . . if I had one." Instead of disappearing, the grin widened. "Fishing, Cassie?"

"No!" she gasped, fighting for composure. "I just thought . . . the ring."

"I *was* married—once."

"Divorced?"

"Does it matter?" Avoiding her question, he advanced to the door, then turned. "Let's just say I'm single again."

"Any children?"

"What is this? Twenty questions?" Though obviously annoyed, his expression suddenly turned thoughtful. "Yes, we had a child . . . a little girl."

"Do you see her often?" Jodi piped in. They had both almost forgotten her presence as she busily rinsed the dishes. "It must be hard with the kind of work you do."

"Harder than you think," he said without a smile. "It's been nearly ten years."

Cassandra wasn't shocked to learn Adam was divorced. She knew imperfect people made imperfect matches, and many were not willing to do what was necessary to make their commitment work. While she couldn't condone divorce, she could understand it. But the abandonment of one's own child was beyond her comprehension. Every child needed the love of both parents, including Adam Ralston's daughter.

"That's terrible!" Jodi exclaimed, nearly dropping the cup she was drying.

"You should be ashamed of yourself! A child . . ."

Cutting Cassandra short, Adam's eyes were like ice. "Save your sermonizing for the natives, ladies." The silence was thick as each stared at the other. "You going to show me that clinic or not—Cassie?"

"Don't call me Cassie!" His use of the familiar form of her name seemed an insult now, no longer to be tolerated. "You aren't George Sanders."

"Nor would I want to be." The muscles of his jaw tightened as he traced the natural lines of Cassandra's face with his eyes. "Yes . . . I can see why George would be interested in you . . . but why would a beautiful young woman be interested in a widower twice her age?"

Cassandra had never seen George Sanders in any other light than confidant and friend. In the two years since Millie's death she and George had become close, but not in the way Adam Ralston obviously believed.

"I don't see it is any of your business, Mr. Ralston." His attitude infuriated her.

"They aren't. . . . She doesn't—" Jodi leapt to her friend's defense.

"Love him?" he finished. "*Do* you love him, Cassandra?"

That twist of a smile was there again, driving her on. "Yes," she answered, her look warning an open-mouthed Jodi to keep quiet. "If you *really* love someone—what difference does age make?"

It was true, she justified. She did love Uncle Geo,

22

but more as a beloved older friend—never in the way she imagined herself loving the man she would someday marry. When she married, *if* she married, it wouldn't be to someone she could live with, but to the one man she couldn't live without—the man in God's plan for her life. This sincere belief had kept her from the altar several times. Cassandra would be content with nothing less.

No one spoke. Nailed to one of the wood supports, the battery-operated clock ticked rhythmically with the accelerated breathing of the room's occupants, contrasting with the faint background noises. The sound of steady pounding filtered through the open window as the women separated the rice from its hulls . . . the cry of a baby . . . the protest of an oxlike carabao being led to the fields . . . only these broke the near-silence. It was still early in the day, but Cassandra felt bone-weary from the emotional toil of their verbal combat, and they hadn't even begun to sort out any of the really important issues.

Cassandra had all but forgotten the two men Adam Ralston had brought with him until one of them suddenly appeared at the door. They had been surveying the general area and now wanted to check with their boss before venturing farther out. Listening to their conversation, she was impressed with Adam's command of the Cebuano language, and wondered if he knew the trade language of Luzon as well. Cassandra had learned both before tackling the more difficult task of becoming conversant in an unwritten language.

As there was now a scant half-hour to show him around and plead her case before Adam was to meet his men, Cassandra suggested they leave on the heels of the Filipinos. Jodi had decided to stay behind, tidy up, and pull out the graded readers she and Cassandra had developed and have them ready for Adam's inspection. Teaching grown men and women such basic skills was difficult, but a vital part of their work if the natives were ever to read God's Word for themselves.

The first stop was the little building that housed the modest clinic. Theirs was not a medical mission, Cassandra explained, but both women had received some training in first aid. The majority of their treatment was for minor injuries and ailments. They dispensed medicine, treated sores, and administered inoculations. It wasn't enough, but it was the only medical help available—except for the local witch doctor. The closest hospital was a long trek to Davao or Butuan.

Cassandra wanted to move on, but Adam walked about the room fingering the equipment and checking the supplies. He said little, but his expression was thoughtful. He seemed to know his way around and Cassandra wondered about his reaction. He was a logger, not a doctor. Though it wasn't customary, Cassandra knew the camp had its own medical facilities, much grander than the mission could afford, and from time to time even a resident doctor.

Robert Howard had been with Pacific Lumber when Cassandra first arrived at the tribe, but the young Australian had left some time ago. He was a fellow Christian and had volunteered his help at the mission. His own job kept him busy, but he did manage at least two visits a month. Many had benefited from his care and the hands-on training he had given Cassandra. This past year she had greatly missed his presence, not only for his medical knowledge, but his personal encouragement as well.

"Did you know Dr. Howard?" she asked Adam impulsively.

"Knew *of* him. Went home to get married and join his father's practice, didn't he? He'd left by the time I came." Tapping the edge of a tray containing readied syringes, he smiled tightly. "Good doctor." Tension showed in his face as he moved his hand away. "Few of them stick it out for very long. I guess that's why the care here is so poor. Your people are better off than most, though," he admitted, almost grudgingly. "We even have a time keeping medical staff at the base. The young ones come for the adventure . . . and the old ones, well, I don't know . . . maybe they come for their last chance at adventure."

"Do you have a doctor now?"

"Yeah," Adam laughed, the lines of his face relaxing. "At least that's what he calls himself. Old Dr. Baker sure didn't come out into the jungle for adventure. I think he came because no one else would have him."

"That bad?" Cassandra grimaced.

"Oh, he can give an injection, set a break, dress a wound. But if I had an attack of appendicitis, I think I'd rather risk the trip to the hospital. If it became inflamed enough to burst, I'd probably stand a better chance at survival with peritonitis than under his scalpel." His lighter mood continued as he spoke. "Of course, I don't have to worry. I had mine out when I was twelve."

"Lucky you!" She had to smile and, when she did, the sparkling blue of her eyes took on new life. "You sound more qualified to answer any questions I might have than your doctor."

"Maybe." Despite the smile that remained, his terse answer gave away his sudden uneasiness. "You won't find Dr. Baker offering any help. We're lucky when we can get him to tend our men in the field. Says the rough roads put his back out."

"Oh," she sympathized, wondering if he'd resented the fact that their former doctor had donated some of his free time to her. "Assure him we don't draft our

25

help. An all-volunteer army works better for everyone."

"The Lord's army." The quote came easily, as did the remembering grin. "As a kid we used to march around singing that song—"

"Then you're a—" she gasped, pleased at the possibility of his being a believer, but puzzled by the instant change of expression her words brought.

"I'm a grown man, Cassandra, not a naïve child who puts on a paper hat and bangs out a worthless tune on the backside of some saucepan." His laugh was bitter. "Only an idealistic fool enlists in an army where the all-powerful Commander-in-Chief entices you with billboards promising love and peace, and then delights in crushing your little world when your back is turned. The price for His love comes too high."

"But, that isn't how God works!" Cassandra marveled at his total misconception of her loving Creator. What could have happened in his life to make him believe all these untruths, she wondered. "Christ—"

Stopping her short, Adam's angry words stunned Cassandra. "You're no different from the rest of them!" She could see the hurt in his eyes, but knew it was the battle raging inside him, and not her words that triggered his outburst. "Christians!" he stated with disgust. "You all think at the name of Christ, the world is supposed to jump. You think life's problems will disappear and all the hurt just melt away. I know better, and sooner or later you'll realize it, too."

"And become like you?" Her voice was barely more than a whisper, her face saddened with concern rather than anger. "I'm a realist, but unlike you, Adam Ralston, I learn from those things God brings into my life. I don't know why you're so bitter, and I'm not even sure *you* do. Christians have the power to change, the power to cope, though we're not guaranteed a problem-free existence." His thoughtful silence encouraged her further. "If you are truly a believer, you can call upon Christ for help in the heat of the battle, but no one has ever won a victory while staging a retreat."

Adam wanted to dismiss her words, but he knew deep inside that what she said was true. For ten years he had been running from God and what he knew he was meant to do. At twenty-eight, life had seemed over for him and he had blamed God. Now this disturbing young woman was making him take a hard look at himself, and he wasn't sure he liked what he saw.

Cassandra's dark blue eyes spoke of her genuine interest, and Adam couldn't erase her image from his mind as he glanced casually at his watch and motioned silently for them to continue the tour. He didn't want to talk about his faith—now or ever. It was too painful and too late, he reasoned, refusing to meet her eyes as they descended the steps together.

CHAPTER 3

HOURS BEFORE DAWN, with only a sliver of a moon to
dispel the inky darkness, Cassandra lay awake listening to the silence. The hungry insects lurking just
beyond her protective netting were her only companions, except for Jodi's rhythmic breathing audible
through the thin bamboo screen separating their
rooms.

For the second night in a row, troubled dreams had
invaded Cassandra's sleep, making it impossible to
retreat into peaceful slumber. Each time the voice of
God had been replaced by the deep, even tones of
Adam Ralston, ordering them from Eden. Only it
hadn't really been Eden. Cassandra shivered as she
recalled the familiar sights of the jungle all around her.
The windows of their home and the little clinic had
been boarded up—left vacant and lifeless. The sad
faces of those trailing behind her haunted her waking
hours as well, and she feared her dreams were only a
prelude to an imminent reality.

Adam had promised to return before the final

decision was reached, but Cassandra doubted he'd been arguing their case before the company's bosses these past two days. She'd seen his plane flying low over the terrain, and felt certain his aerial survey was for the purpose of making the logging company's plans, having already dismissed the mission's cause due to her blundering. If she was correct, Pacific Lumber would soon be moving in, and they would be moving out!

Restless inside her cocoon, Cassandra threw back her coverings and lit the oil lamp beside her bed. Being careful not to wake Jodi, she made her way to the kitchen, hoping a hot cup of tea might help to calm her nerves and rid her mind of thoughts of Adam Ralston.

Instead of erasing his image, the warm brew brought back the memory of Adam's visit. His arrogance had angered her then, but it wasn't his arrogance that bothered her now. Cassandra knew her sleeplessness wasn't solely caused by her concern for the future of the mission. The relocation of the tribe would make the job of reaching them more difficult, but not impossible. No, what frightened her most was this unshakable attraction she was feeling for a man she barely knew and didn't even like.

Knowing she had to rest, Cassandra took a last swallow of her tea and rinsed the cup before resuming her attempt at sleep. She was to work in the clinic in a few hours and needed to be alert. The patient load had increased in recent months, not because of illness among members of the tribe, but because of their greater confidence in the young missionaries. Though the majority were still not ready to accept Cassandra's and Jodi's God, many more were accepting their medical help. For some the *Datu* still wielded the final authority. Others, having seen for themselves the clinic's results, no longer believed all illness and misfortune was linked to spirit appeasement. Datu

Salvador's prescribed remedy of sacrificing pigs and chickens was slowly being replaced with antibiotics and aspirin, while each failure to heal was heralded by the tribal leader as the spirits' revenge on the unfaithful. The number of "unfaithful" grew, and Cassandra slipped back into her room confident someday that even crusty old Salvador would join the ranks.

The tightly wound cargo released like a paper streamer hurled at a departing ship. Cassandra had to smile along with the two giggling children as they watched the roll of gauze bandages speed across the clinic floor. "That's enough, Dominic." The sternness of her words was not mirrored in the blue haven of her eyes as she scolded the sun-browned urchin. "How do you expect me to change the dressing on your brother's leg if you ruin my supplies before I even get to him?"

The contrite expression on the seven-year-old's saucer face was well rehearsed, but less than genuine. "*Manang* forgives?" Dominic knew his calling Cassandra "older sister" would gain him a more favorable audience. It was what all the young ones called her, but in his case it had a broader meaning—she was his spiritual sister as well.

Fely's younger grandson, Miguel, sat quietly waiting to hear Cassandra's reply. She knew he respected Dominic's ability to talk his way out of anything, singularly lacking in that valuable skill himself. Since the time their grandmother began to believe in just the "one" Spirit, neither child had been allowed to tell the lies so accepted in their culture. It mattered little where Miguel was concerned, however, for his wide teddy bear eyes always betrayed him.

Even among a people where an adult male much over five feet was considered huge, Miguel was small for his five years. It was his constant effort to prove himself to his peers that made him a regular customer of the clinic. Only yesterday he had been showing off with his father's machete, missing the bamboo stalk but not his leg. The cut was minor as injuries go, but Cassandra had seen less than that take a life when infection was allowed to set in and the wound remained untreated.

Scooping up the soiled cloth, Cassandra deposited it in the trash and then turned back to her expectant patient. "*Manang* forgives," she smiled, knowing that only a few weeks ago Dominic had learned from Fely the meaning of true forgiveness. "But that innocent look won't save you from the vaccination your mother sent you in here for."

Giving shots to children was the least favorite part of her job, although some of the adults carried on more than the smallest infant. The brave set of Dominic's jaw told Cassandra he would not cry in front of his brother. Dominic took seriously his job of setting an example, especially since the arrival of the new baby and the longer hours his father was putting in in the field. As the eldest son of the family, he was determined to do his part.

"*Manang!* " the half-dressed little girl called excitedly, startling everyone as the door was suddenly flung open. "The logger man is coming!"

"What?" Cassandra gasped, nearly dropping the vial she was holding.

"Adam's in the clearing." Jodi burst in from the rear.

Freeing her hands, Cassandra glanced over her old *mahlong*, self-consciously retying the securing knot of the loose-fitting garment. "I *should* change."

"Maybe . . ." Jodi conceded, noting how the fresh stains on Cassandra's *mahlong* blended with the old ones, together creating their own secondary pattern. "But there's no time," she reasoned. "He'll just have to take us the way he finds us."

32

"You're right!" Cassandra stated stubbornly. "He has easy communication with Butuan. He could have told the mission he was coming and they would have informed us when they radioed last night, or even this morning." Smiling tightly at Dominic, Cassandra went back to the job of administering his inoculation. "Mr. Ralston can just wait his turn."

"And how long will that be . . . Miss Wellsley?"

Sharply alerted to his presence, Cassandra turned toward the voice that had haunted her dreams. Adam Ralston was even more handsome than she'd remembered. Unable to take her eyes from his, she stared into their pale blue depths, momentarily forgetting that four other pairs of eyes were witnessing this intimate exchange.

"I'll put the 'closed' sign up," Jodi volunteered, motioning for Adam to come into the room. "Let's go, Miguel, Dominic. You can see Cassandra later."

"No," Adam declared, ignoring the relieved sigh that came from the older boy as he prepared to jump down from the examining table. "Keep the others out, but Cassandra and I will finish up here."

"You?" she questioned.

"You?" Jodi echoed, surprised by the positive shake of Adam's head. "I'll . . . um . . . I'll see both of you later," she faltered, obeying Adam's silent command to leave along with the native girl who helped in the clinic.

Once the door was closed, Adam picked up a trusting Miguel and deposited him on the opposite end of the hard wooden table. "Had an accident, have you?" Gently lifting the beaming child's leg, Adam began to unwrap the once-white bandage. "What happened?"

"He told us he was harvesting bamboo so he could build his own house."

"That so?" Adam laughed, his large hand ruffling

Miguel's already untidy shock of black hair. "Next time maybe you should look for a smaller machete."

"You doctor?" Dominic chimed in, using two of the dozen or so English words in his vocabulary.

"No," Cassandra answered for him. "This is Adam Ralston from the lumber company."

"Logger man!"

"Sorry . . ." Cassandra could feel the blush build beneath her tan. "I'm afraid that's what they all call you around here."

"I've been called worse!" The lines of Adam's face grew more pronounced as his grin widened, fleetingly displaying his dimple.

Cassandra watched as Adam cleaned the wound and helped himself to the supplies. His touch was surprisingly gentle, and he was tender and attentive, causing her to wonder afresh how he could have gone for ten years without seeing his own child.

"Looks good," he complimented, referring to the initial treatment. "Ever consider becoming a nurse?"

"No," she smiled, drawing back on the syringe. "But when I run into problems I can't handle here, I often wish I were a doctor."

"Ouch!" Dominic exclaimed, forgetting to be brave.

"Off with you," Cassandra laughed, putting a bandage over the site. "And don't forget to tell your mother to bring the baby in next week."

Finishing up with Miguel, Adam lifted the youngster high into the air before setting him down and giving him a playful pat on the rear. "Go on," he prompted, gazing pensively after the two brothers as they scurried out the door. "Cute little rascals," he declared, watching as they ran down the path toward their home.

Having logged the latest treatments in her record book, Cassandra smiled her agreement. "It's only been in this last year their mother has allowed them to come to the clinic. Listening to the *Datu* cost her two children, so when Miguel came down with pneumonia, his grandmother sent for me. By that time the mother was too worried to refuse. He got better, so now the whole family comes."

Crossing the room, Adam swung the remaining chair around and straddled its back. His large frame dwarfed the small furnishing, straining at the strawlike bindings as he leaned forward, "Had much trouble with the *Datu?*"

"Not at first," Cassandra admitted, remembering how Salvador had welcomed them and even offered his daughter Marta to teach them the language. "He wanted the easy outside trade for his people, the clothes missionaries always give, and the cast-off cans and containers. They always need cans, it seems. They use them for bowls, cooking pots—everything."

Noticing the supplies still out of place, she rose and placed them in the cabinet so they'd be there when she needed them again. "He even approved of the clinic! He'd heard if we stuck people with a special needle it made the spirits happy and those people wouldn't get sick."

That now familiar crooked smile greeted Cassandra as she rejoined Adam. "So where's the problem?"

"There wasn't any," Cassandra explained, "until we learned enough of the language to tell the people about the 'one' Spirit."

Adam's smile vanished. The flimsy chair moaned in protest as he shifted his weight, nervously running a hand through his silver hair. "Well, I'd love to hear more, but I came here to talk to you about my recommendation. I spoke with the company yesterday and the news isn't good."

Cassandra's face paled. Salvador and his use of fear to retain his control over the people was not her immediate problem. The reality of her nightmare was

35

beginning. She wasn't sure which hurt more—the village's relocation, or Adam's failure to defend them. The last few minutes had been spent so pleasantly she had begun to hope he was going to fight for their right to stay.

"You okay?"

His false concern angered her. "Fine," she lied.

"Sure? Your color's getting better, but for a second there you looked like you might faint."

"I never faint!" Refusing his offer of a hand, she got up and went to the rear door. "If you'll follow me to the house, I'd like to change—"

"You look fine," he asserted. "Except maybe for this—" Reaching behind Cassandra, Adam released the clip holding back her hair. Long, honey-colored strands were forced free as he lifted the silken mass with his hand. "That's better."

Shaken by his actions, Cassandra turned away and walked absently down the steps, almost forgetting her destination. If Adam were the man she thought him to be, then her attraction for him was wrong. She couldn't let Adam see into the deep blue of her eyes— the windows of her soul. His touch had renewed in Cassandra the inner turmoil that had been raging practically from the moment of their meeting.

Who was this man she seemed so unable to resist? Was Adam Ralston the gentle giant who cared for the children of a stranger, or the callous father who had deserted his own daughter? Where did the truth lie? Did he really believe he had a rational reason for turning his back on the God Cassandra loved and was determined to serve? Or was he, like so many others, using any excuse to deny God, so he could serve only himself? Cassandra wished she knew.

CHAPTER 4

Catching up, Adam grabbed Cassandra's arm, halting her progress. "Where do you think you're going?"

"To change," she stated weakly, all the fight drained from her. Usually self-assured, Cassandra hoped maybe a pair of slacks and a fresh blouse might make her feel more comfortable. She wasn't looking forward to hearing what Adam had to say.

"Do it later."

A group of curiosity-seekers had gathered, and, not wishing to create a scene, Cassandra had no choice but to accompany Adam. Still holding her arm, he led her past the main clearing and on down a well-traveled trail to a smaller, more remote clearing. Delicately hued orchids hung from the tree next to the fallen log where he motioned for her to sit. Under normal circumstances she would have thought it quite pleasant, but Cassandra was too tense to enjoy the aesthetics.

Though only a short distance away, the village sounds no longer intruded, being replaced by the primitive music of wild creatures. A brightly plumed bird flew overhead, crying out a ritual mating call. The sweet smell of freshly bloomed jasmine mingled with the musty odor of a constantly decaying forest. Ample foliage shielded them from most of the sun's rays, but they couldn't escape the ever-present humidity.

"I saw this spot on my way in today," Adam explained. "It seemed a good place to hold a private conversation."

Forced to look at him, Cassandra said nothing, her throat too tight for words.

"Okay," he sighed, lowering his body onto the stump opposite Cassandra. His narrowed eyes searched her face for answers, but found none. "Let's have it."

Picking at a twig that had become lodged in her sandals, Cassandra averted her eyes once more, wondering what Adam expected her to say. Had he anticipated that she would take the news without getting upset?

Her continued silence angered him more. "Look at me!" he demanded. "I didn't come all this way today to have you ignore me. I thought we were being pretty civilized back there in the clinic, but evidently I was wrong. If you're going to be mad at me, then at least tell me what I've done."

"I'd hoped . . ." Cassandra began, strong emotion preventing her from continuing.

"I know. . . ." With a heavy sigh, Adam shifted on the stump. "You're disappointed about the logging operation . . . But remember, I'm not the one who makes the decisions. Carlos Valdez is the company head, not I."

"I know that," Cassandra sniffed softly, the hurt in her eyes there for him to see. "But . . . if you . . . I thought maybe . . ."

Lifting his hand to her cheek, he wiped away the moisture. "You crying?"

"No," she lied, pushing his hand aside. "I never cry!"

A raised eyebrow challenged her reply. "Then it must be rain," he stated dryly, moving over to sit next to her on the log. "Here," he offered her his handkerchief.

"I don't need it," she protested through her tears as he placed a comforting arm around her shoulder.

"Go ahead," he encouraged, cradling Cassandra in his arms and rocking her as he would a child in distress. "Go ahead and cry."

Being in Adam's embrace was exhilarating. For the first time Cassandra felt that she had met someone with whom she wanted to belong. But she knew a lasting relationship between them was not possible, not even if her growing conviction were true—that Adam's divorce and separation from his daughter had somehow been forced upon him. But that wasn't the *real* issue between them. The real issue was one of faith—and the fact that they seemed to be poles apart in their beliefs. Still, it felt good to be here in his arms, however briefly, and she allowed herself to savor the moment.

Though her tears were subsiding, Adam held her even tighter.

"Don't give up hope," he admonished aloud. "I haven't. I'm sure that after Valdez and his men meet you at the party on Friday, they'll reconsider my recommendation to explore another site."

"What party?" she questioned, not daring to believe her ears. "I'm not going to any party. There's no time . . ." she protested, pulling away and drying her eyes.

"Well, you'll have to go if you're to prove you aren't some incompetent female."

39

"What?"

"You'll understand when you've met them," he explained soothingly. "They're old school and they don't want to waste a lot of time and money, just so a couple of old maids can play queen of the jungle."

"You told them—" she attempted.

"No," he laughed. "That's what *they* believe. They think all women should be married and home having babies. They really aren't a bad group of men."

"You told them to—to move the site?" she finally got out.

"Sure," he puzzled, his brows knitting as he reviewed his words. "Didn't I say that?"

"No," she answered, smiling shyly. "I thought—"

"You thought I'd told them to go ahead with the relocation?" The shake of her head confirmed it. "So that's why you were so angry with me!"

"Exactly." Bending forward, Cassandra broke off a small lavender bloom from one of the low-lying plants near her feet, relieved Adam was on their side. The wild orchid danced in the air as she absently twisted the slender stem between her fingers. "After making a disaster out of our first meeting, I really held out little hope . . . until today." Peering up at the man whose arms she had just left, she suddenly felt awkward. "I don't think I ever thanked you for your help in the clinic today . . . maybe you're the one who should have been a doctor."

"Forget it," he dismissed, his smile suddenly tight. "It was nothing."

Cassandra recognized that warning look—she had seen it before. Its unspoken caution dared her to trespass into the inner sanctum of his soul. The limits were clearly posted, and she knew pushing would only damage their already tenuous relationship. Taboo were the subjects of his family, God, and medicine, making her wonder if somehow together they formed the key to unlocking the real Adam Ralston.

Rising, Adam took Cassandra's hand and pulled her to her feet. "I'll tell you about the party on the walk back."

In her excitement, his other words had barely registered, but she knew no invitation had actually been issued. "Don't you ever ask, instead of just ordering?" she demanded, with slight annoyance.

"Sometimes," he admitted, an infuriating smile playing at the edges of his mouth. "I've found when you tell people to do something—they usually do it. Giving them a choice causes confusion. Most people are natural followers."

There was some logic in his statement, but none Cassandra cared to acknowledge. "Is that the way you see *me*?"

"No, . . ." The blue of his eyes sparkled as he recalled their first meeting. "You only follow the leaders you've chosen, and then only if you believe what they're telling you to do is right . . . and I doubt if even that comes naturally to you."

"Now you're making me sound difficult!" she pouted, pausing as they began their short journey back to the village.

"But not impossible." Adam's grin widened as he studied her expression. "Come on," he motioned. "If you'd been any different, I just might have been inclined to agree with my company boss. Being part Spaniard, he is used to his women at least playing the helpless role—unable to function adequately without a man."

"Spanish, too!" Cassandra pondered, stepping up her pace. "He sounds like the kind who believes women are strong enough physically for hard labor, but too weak mentally to make their own decisions. . . . Thanks for the warning!"

"Maybe it's Carlos Valdez who should be warned," Adam laughed, the thought pleasing him. "I have a feeling he's in for a *big* surprise!"

The damp, humid climate of the jungle was no place for the delicate fabrics of the lovely dresses that lay across Cassandra's bed, awaiting her choice. Normally they were stored along with a few of her other belongings at the mission's guest house in Manila, but a few months earlier she had brought them back here.

The organization had grown so over the years that the original building could no longer adequately house the many guests to the field or the workers when they came in from the surrounding areas for conferences. The facility was to be enlarged, and the mission was concerned that, with all the confusion and outside help, something might be lost or stolen. At the time it had seemed a nuisance to lug her heavy trunk back to the compound with her, but Cassandra was thankful now she had the outfits on hand.

Occasionally she did get an opportunity to dress up, and she knew her aunt would be highly offended if she heard her Christmas gifts were hanging in a closet in a New Orleans suburb. Cassandra suspected that the expensive clothes, along with the monthly stack of fashion magazines, were calculated to make her miss the "good" life and return to the fold where Ernestine Powers felt she belonged.

"Which one are you taking?" Jodi asked, a finger tracing the spiral quilt patterns on the bright aqua jacket. The cool feel of silk greeted her touch, her eyes wandering on to the matching skirt and contrasting accordion-pleated blouse. "This is lovely!"

"They all are," Cassandra sighed, picking up the golden tan crepe de Chine. The glass-beaded border sparkled as it reflected the morning sun. "My aunt has great taste."

Standing in front of the small mirror, Cassandra held the dress to her. "He said 'after-five', but I don't want to overdress."

"Then wear this one," Jodi urged, pointing to the remaining dress. "It's sophisticated, but still very feminine. I've always loved a ruffled neck. Let's see . . . somewhere I have a pendant that's just about that shade of rose. . . ." Her expression thoughtful, she relieved Cassandra of the delicate crepe and held the full-skirted chiffon up for her to see. "No . . ." she amended, "I'd leave it just as it is, no jewelry . . . except for your thin gold chain bracelet. Try it on."

The rich satiny lining slid deliciously over Cassandra's body as she jockeyed Jodi's choice into position. Fastening the sheer sleeves at her wrists, she tightened the belt and stepped back. The length was traditional, displaying her shapely calves below the hemline. It was romantic, but not frilly.

"I like it," she smiled, allowing her hand to caress its conservative V neckline, the folds of gossamer material cascading down almost to her waist. Removing the dress, Cassandra carefully folded it into her pack. "Adam said the guest house is pretty modern. It will be nice to have hot running water and plug-in curlers for a change."

"Electricity isn't everything!"

"No," Cassandra laughed, slipping back into her faded jeans and T-shirt. "But I doubt that one night is going to spoil me much."

"If someone like Adam Ralston invited me to fly with him to Butuan so I could be his date for a party, I'd be spoiled for life." The impish grin on Jodi's face didn't diminish under Cassandra's stare.

"It wasn't exactly an invitation," she reminded her friend. "I'd call it a command performance . . . and it isn't a date. . . ."

"No?"

"You know what I mean!" Placing the last few items in her bag, she zipped it closed. "Why don't you make yourself useful and ask Fely if Bobbit is about ready to leave."

Choosing her own form of usefulness, Jodi carefully replaced the other two outfits. "You should have taken Adam up on his offer to come down the trail for you, then you could have spent the two hours talking to him instead of taking poor Bobbit away from his work."

"Poor Bobbit!" she gasped. "It was you who asked him to escort me!"

"Well, you couldn't go alone."

Taking hold of the lightweight frame, Cassandra moved her gear out to the front door. "I guess not," she admitted reluctantly. Filling her canteen with preboiled water, she glanced over at the red nylon carrier, then, ruefully at her faded jeans. "I look more like a Girl Scout going on a camp-out than a respectable young woman attending a four-star party."

Jodi puzzled over Cassandra's words, not because they weren't true, but because in her three years with her she had never seen Cassandra so preoccupied with her appearance. At times her teammate had almost seemed to resent her natural beauty. Something was definitely in the air. . . .

As planned, Adam was parked at the end of the trail, waiting to take them to the airplane. Whatever fatigue Cassandra had suffered en route vanished when she saw Adam's familiar figure. He stepped briskly from the Jeep to relieve Bobbit of the backpack and help her in. The morning sun hadn't been as hot as she'd feared, but more than once she and Bobbit had stopped to take sips of the tepid water they both carried. Cool images of ice cubes clinking against frosted glasses filled her head as she thought of the party she'd be attending in a few short hours.

Waving her thanks to the brightly smiling native, she got in, wondering how long it would take Bobbit to make it back to the village. Jodi's concern about taking him away from his work had been almost laughable. Bobbit was known to be notoriously lazy when it came to his duties as a farmer. He never seemed to tire of fishing and hunting, or even the job of cutting wood for the houses, but the burning off of the fields to prepare for planting and the ultimate harvesting were another story.

During their drive Adam's eyes returned frequently to the smooth lines of Cassandra's face, the vivid blue of her eyes, and the strands of darkened gold that danced in the artificial breeze of motion. It had been ten years since he had allowed himself to care. He'd thought his heart was sealed forever after being forced to give up the woman and child he loved, but he hadn't counted on someone like Cassandra.

While she would be taking her time dressing for the party, he would be fighting to keep her physically near him. But even if the meeting with his boss went well, he knew he would be helpless to lessen the gap between their souls. He understood Cassandra far better than she knew, and it was because of this understanding that he felt certain nothing lasting could ever develop between them. The kindest thing for them both would be never to see her again—but that would require greater strength then he possessed.

CHAPTER 5

NATIVE-GROWN NARRA WOOD PANELING graced the walls, giving the room a distinctively masculine flavor. Even the forest green of the draperies was more suited to a man's taste than to a woman's. Considering the nature of the work at the processing plant, Cassandra doubted that much thought was given to female guests, considering that their percentage was very small.

Earlier, voices reverberating through the narrow hall had alerted her to the arrival of others, the clicking of high heels on the wooden planks oddly reassuring. She would have hated being the only woman present tonight.

The knock on the door came as no surprise. Cassandra was expecting Adam's summons. She'd dressed early, knowing he wanted her to meet those who would determine the fate of the mission before the others arrived.

"Coming." Nervously Cassandra glanced once more at the mirror. She had wanted to look her best, and she did. It had been years since she'd made the effort. Silently she prayed all would go well. Taking a deep breath, she turned the handle. "How did—" Cassandra's words stuck in her throat. The black eyes greeting her bore no resemblance to the cool blue ones she had anticipated.

The beautiful Filipina took in every inch of Cassandra, from the lush curls of her head to the expensive dyed leather of the shoes her aunt had sent to complete the rose chiffon outfit. "*You* —the missionary?"

The young woman's tone bordered on reproach, as if she were accusing Cassandra of role-playing. "Yes, I'm Cassandra Wellsley—"

"I know." Cutting her short, she sailed past Cassandra and into the room, uninvited. The scent of her perfume lingered as she crossed over to the bed. "I was sent by Adam and my father to see if you were ready to join them."

"Then you're—"

"Triana Valdez," she finished for her, sitting on the edge of the bed and fingering the glass beads of Cassandra's purse. With eyes narrowed she surveyed Cassandra once more. "Shall I tell them you'll be awhile yet?"

Adam had mentioned there was a daughter, but he had spoken as if she were still in the schoolroom. His time-warped opinion did not fit the very sophisticated Miss Valdez who stood before her now. "I'm ready," Cassandra answered, monitoring her voice to conceal the fact she had caught the other woman's veiled barb.

Triana made no move toward the door. Instead, she picked up Cassandra's evening bag by its thin silver chain, twisting the body and then allowing it to spin freely. Dropping the temporary plaything on the bed, she sat silently.

Cassandra watched, not wanting to offend the host's daughter, but eager to leave the room. The tension between them was real, though Cassandra couldn't imagine a cause. "Your father and Adam are waiting," she reminded Triana, the numbers on her watch attesting to the fact that the other guests would be arriving in less than half an hour. "I'm sure I could find my own way if you have things to do."

Cassandra's offer was dismissed with a shake of Triana's head, her shiny, black mane contrasting brilliantly with the bright red of her high-necked dress. Rising, she handed Cassandra her purse. "I will present you ... I am my father's hostess this evening."

"Then your mother will not be joining us?" The question brought a frown to Triana's youthful face, making Cassandra wish back her words.

"The present Mrs. Valdez is *not* my mother." The matter-of-fact statement was delivered in flawless English. "Margarita hates to fly, so since my return from college I have been taking her place. She's at my father's home in Manila."

Cassandra hadn't suspected there was a stepmother, but given his own circumstances, she doubted Adam would have found the information relevant. It was clear to Cassandra that Triana resented her mother's replacement. Was her real mother dead? Divorced? Divorce was frowned upon, but not altogether unknown among the sometimes highly religious elite class of the Philippines. Being an only child, it would have been quite difficult for Triana to have accepted anyone, Cassandra realized, especially if Carlos Valdez had waited some years before remarrying.

"Margarita urged me to return to the States for further study, but I am finished with school." Triana's voice held a bitter edge as she spoke of her step-

49

mother. "What I want is right here in the Philippines, and *no one* is going to stand in my way."

Dark eyes flashed as she turned to glare at Cassandra, daring her to ask what it was Triana desired so passionately.

"Many years I have waited," she began, walking as far as the door. "What I want . . . no," she corrected, her expression daring Cassandra to challenge her. "What I *will have* is . . . Adam Ralston.

Riotous thoughts crowded Cassandra's head as she followed in Triana's wake, down the stairs and over to the large room where the festivities would soon begin. There had been nothing to say. Was Adam interested in Triana, or was it all one-sided? He could do worse than the boss's daughter, she had to admit. Triana was beautiful, intelligent, and wealthy, though maybe a trifle young.

All eyes focused on the two women as they entered the room, passed the serving table laden with local dishes, and continued on to the far corner of the room where four men stood talking. "I have brought her," Triana announced, not bothering to make the proper introductions.

Cassandra's attention was naturally drawn to Adam, the carefully tailored lines of his navy suit setting well upon his lean torso. "You look wonderful," he breathed. "I'll have to bring you out of the jungle more often."

Without speaking, they spoke. But Cassandra feared in the end it would be a sad song, best left unwritten. Even if Triana meant nothing to him, her road to happiness—and Adam's—seemed destined to lead in very different directions. What he offered she couldn't take, not without losing herself. She knew all this—had known from the beginning—but knowledge, her faithful ally, was proving impotent in the face of strong emotion. Only by the grace of God would she be able to remain poised on this precipice. God had promised not to allow temptation beyond what she could bear, but strong winds and strange voices called for her to plunge over the edge. To soar, to float in the arms of love, forgetting for a space of time the realities below.

She knew Scripture admonished one to flee at times like these, but all she could manage was caution. Did circumstances or God keep throwing her in Adam Ralston's path? Was her limited vision keeping her from seeing His plan, or was it only wishful thinking on her part, an attempt to justify what she was beginning to want so desperately?

These thoughts plagued her as she tore her gaze from Adam and politely acknowledged the presence of the other three gentlemen. "Delighted," she heard as an echo, vaguely recognizing that the voice was her own.

As expected, the oldest was Carlos Valdez. Taller than most Filipinos, his unusual height gave him a distinguished presence. The two younger men by his side mirrored their boss's expression, gazing admiringly at Cassandra. Unlike the tribals, these men were sophisticated enough to appreciate such an international beauty.

"You were wrong not to warn us," Carlos Valdez scolded Adam good-naturedly. "Miss Wellsley will think our reception rude. . . ."

Adam threw a conspiratorial smile Cassandra's way. "I wanted to surprise you. . . . Cassandra's beauty was the one thing upon which I knew we wouldn't disagree."

"Only she is more beautiful than any words could express," Carlos stated in agreement. "Rarely do we see such a jewel of womanhood toiling alone in a valley of banana trees and stilted huts."

"I have a partner," she corrected.

"I meant, of course, that you have no husband."

Only her prior knowledge of Carlos Valdez's opinion of women saved Cassandra from saying something that would cement his limited view forever.

"Even the mission prefers couples," she admitted, sensing it was best to agree with him in principle, while proving to him the exception was often workable. "There are more tribes than couples willing to work with them, however, and I'm sure you would agree a single man and a single woman would make an inappropriate mission team."

"Certainly," he gasped. "I didn't mean to suggest—"

"I know," Cassandra smiled, taking advantage of his sudden state of confusion to press her point. "But without those couples, singles of the same sex are the only answer." Silence ensued as the logging president considered the truth of her words. "Our main task is to translate the Bible into the language of the natives and to establish a church run by one of their own. A man *or* a woman can accomplish that."

Adam gave her an encouraging smile as she paused to consider how far her arguments should go. "We aren't a medical mission, but our presence does guarantee an improved standard of living and basic health care for many people. Surely you are in sympathy with these objectives?"

This wasn't a new banner, Cassandra realized, but one her mission and others had used successfully many times. Though most of the companies they dealt with cared little about the spiritual aspect of the work, many could rally around the educational and medical welfare of the natives. Poverty and ignorance bred discontent, and any efforts at alleviating it were welcomed, regardless of the source.

Cassandra knew that, like most in his class, Mr.

Valdez would belong to philanthropic organizations. Her hope was he would aid their cause in an effort to display his generosity more directly. Selecting a new site would mean investment of capital, but his outlay couldn't begin to compare with the mission's loss if the logging company's present plans were carried out.

"We at the mission realize it would be unrealistic to ask that you never clear the valley in which our tribe resides." *Perhaps compromise is the best we can hope for*, Cassandra mused. "With the present unrest in the Philippines and the rebel control of such vast areas, the additional five to ten years originally projected is probably too much to ask . . . but won't you consider delaying the project as long as possible?"

Carlos Valdez's eyes drifted to Adam and then, admiringly, back to her. "I can see my friend here left out more than just the fact of your beauty. . . . I will consider your words."

"So here you are!" The heavy Australian accent diverted their attention. Strolling confidently into the room, the new arrival placed his order with the bartender before extending his hand to the other men. He smiled broadly as he caught a glimpse of Cassandra. "Sorry I'm late." Though his remarks were addressed to the group, his gaze never strayed from her face.

The sound of a bell alerted them to the arrival of several other guests. "That will be Juan and Dodong," the blond man informed them. "I saw them on my way over." Accepting his drink, the unabashed Aussie took a sip and then offered to secure one for Cassandra.

"No, thanks," she declined politely, watching as Carlos and Triana Valdez left to perform their duties as hosts. It was a relief no longer to have Triana's dark eyes boring into her, censoring every word. "I'll

53

have some punch a little later," she concluded, hoping she hadn't offended him with her refusal.

The handsome stranger laughed good-naturedly. "I can see ol' Adam here has finally taken my advice . . . I told him to forget the past and find himself a new woman." The remaining two Filipinos looked on, their fixed smiles seemed empty, telling Cassandra they understood very little of the English being spoken. "Though I can't figure out how he could have found someone as lovely as you here in Mindanao. . . . But now that he has, I might just have to do a little pilfering." The devil dancing in the blue of his eyes decried any serious intentions in his words. "But I can't be stealing you away from him until we've been properly introduced."

Laughing at his friend's outrageous behavior, Adam placed an arm loosely around Cassandra's shoulders. "Jonathan, I've been telling you you needed to get out into the jungle more often—you'd be surprised at what you might find."

"A rare monkey and a bunch of rotten bananas, if I know my luck! Or maybe that poor, old-maid missionary you were supposed to bring out to plead her cause!" Cassandra and Adam exchanged looks, but Jonathan Sloan was having too much fun with his imaginary accounting to notice. "Not that I can blame you for dumping her to bring this stunning lass . . . if the Bible boys didn't snap her up before she hit the ground running, she must have a face only a mother could love."

Tears of laughter trickled down Cassandra's face as she anticipated Jonathan Sloan's reaction when he learned the truth of her identity. A grin so wide it tested the muscles of Adam's mouth threatened to spill over into uncontrolled mirth. And the expressions of the two Filipinos only added to the hilarious scenario.

The room was beginning to fill with people, the chatter of mixed languages masking the sound of their dual laughter. A bewildered Jonathan asked them what they'd found so humorous. He'd played it for a laugh, but even he knew his words did not merit this kind of reaction.

From the corner of her eye, Cassandra noticed Carlos Valdez, making his way back to them. Taking a tissue from her bag, she quickly tried to repair the damage done to her make-up, while attempting to suppress a fresh wave of giggles. Nudging Adam, she almost lost the battle as she witnessed his own efforts at control.

"I can see, Miss Wellsley, that you have met our flamboyant plant manager," Mr. Valdez opened.

"She sure has," Adam chuckled.

Cassandra could see the light of knowledge begin to dawn as her name was mentioned. "Isn't that the—" Jonathan gasped.

"So what do you think of our missionary?" prompted Adam.

Triana joined the group just as Adam was offering Cassandra the use of his large handkerchief. The few scraps of tissue she held balled in her hand could not even begin to do the job. Tears when she laughed had always been an embarrassment, but Cassandra had learned long ago it was futile to fight the inevitable.

Dabbing at the faint smudges she knew would be under her eyes, she tried to ignore Triana's hateful glare. She was well aware of the reason; the girl couldn't have made it plainer. But there was no way Cassandra could disengage herself gracefully from Adam's arm, draped casually across her shoulders— even if she'd wanted to.

If she wanted to. Cassandra mulled the thought over in her head. Even with the knowledge that there was nothing behind the gesture, Adam's strong arm felt reassuring. She liked the idea of their being friends, though deep inside she hoped they could somehow be much more.

The full moon shining over the garden beckoned. Cassandra had excused herself early from the party, but sleep eluded her. In her restlessness she'd listened as each guest departed, or retired for the night. The conversation between Carlos Valdez and his daughter as they'd passed her door, and the eerie silence now pervading the old house, told her she was probably one of the few still awake. Most of the guests, including Adam, had a morning meeting, but she didn't really have to make an appearance until lunch, after which she would be flying back to the base with him.

Slipping into her jeans, Cassandra silently stole down the dark hall and out into the cool early-morning air. Bright stars illuminated the weathered stone bench beneath the fernlike foliage of a graceful royal poinciana. Even though the tree's brilliant scarlet blooms were a feast to her eyes, they did little to lift her spirits. She watched the flickering torches bordering the path, each fighting for a last moment of life. The main floodlights had been extinguished long before, not that they'd ever really been needed.

Faint city sounds, the purr of a distant automobile seeming almost foreign, were the only indications of the world outside the walls of the compound. Cassandra was inescapably alone with her thoughts. Honesty forced her to admit it hadn't been only the presence of Triana that had driven her from the festivities. Adam had paid the younger woman scant attention, except in the bantering style of an older brother or favorite uncle, and Cassandra doubted he saw the beautiful Triana as much more than a child. But the realization he might someday open his eyes to her obvious charms was a jolt. No. She was jealous, and she knew it.

All night, she had tried to excuse her unsettled emotions as just the natural competition between two attractive women, but Cassandra knew it was more— much more. She cared for Adam Ralston in a way she had never cared for any other man. It was hopeless, so the practical side of her nature dictated. But her heart said differently.

Absorbed in her own thoughts, Cassandra failed to hear the soft footsteps on the moonlit path. When Adam appeared before her, she thought for a moment he must be a projection of her conscious thoughts. An illusion. Wasn't the real Adam Ralston asleep in the room at the other end of the hall from her own? She had heard him come up the stairs; she knew he had gone to bed. Was this phantom just a product of her growing fatigue?

"Hello," Adam ventured, her expression warning him of her preoccupation. "You okay?"

A smile crept across Cassandra's face; a silent invitation, into her eyes. He lowered himself onto the bench. She marvelled at how real it all seemed, extending her hand to gently follow the contours of his rugged face.

"Cassandra . . ." Adam intercepted her hand and brought it to his lips. Drawing her to him, he murmured against her ear. "My sweet, sweet Cassandra."

"Adam!" she gasped suddenly, pushing him away. "No!" Cassandra pleaded, as he tried to bring her back into his embrace. "I thought . . . I didn't think . . ."

"Which is it?" Adam asked, a distinct edge to his words. "Who *did* you think I was?"

"No one!" she answered sharply, rising to her feet. How could she explain? Her mind raced, conflicting emotions clouding her perception. She had to hang on to her resolve. Any relationship with Adam Ralston could only spell disaster. It wouldn't even work if by some miracle he returned her love. Love was more than a feeling, it was a decision. She refused to love Adam and abandon herself and her God. She could live without Adam Ralston, because she knew she had to.

There was nothing to say. Cassandra turned in the direction of the house, but her parting words were lost as Adam stayed her exit. Turning her around, he pinioned her arms while his eyes searched her face. She wanted to lean against him and surrender to his kiss. But in this war there were no small battles she could afford to lose without sacrificing more than she could ever regain.

"I wish I'd been the one you were thinking of," Adam stated softly, his tone one of regret.

Cassandra wanted so to tell him *he* had been the man in her thoughts, the reason for her inability to sleep. It was Adam Ralston who was the tempter in her garden. He was almost irresistible, making what she knew to be wrong seem so right.

"You're beautiful!" Releasing her arms, he cupped her face, forcing her to look at him. "Why do you have to be so beautiful?"

Why, indeed? Cassandra thought. If she had been the homely woman Jonathan Sloan had expected, she would never have attracted the attention of a man like Adam. Would Adam have championed their cause if she had been unattractive? The fate of the mission was still undecided, but she felt optimistic. Cassandra often wondered if their mutual attraction had ultimately been the cause of his about-face, or if it had been the reason for his initial rejection.

Adam suddenly released her with an oath, turning his back this time. "George Sanders is a fool!"

"What?" Cassandra had forgotten all about that little charade. Did he still believe she loved George?

"Does he know his girl sits alone on a garden bench at two o'clock in the morning, pining for him? The man deserves to lose you."

"But—" she objected.

"Do you deny you wish he were here?"

"No. . . ." More than Adam knew, she wished Uncle Geo were here in Butuan. She needed to talk to him. He would tell her what to do. He would encourage her to do what she knew to be right, instead of what she wanted to be right.

"It's late," Adam barked, glancing at his watch. "I saw you from my window and came down to bring you back inside. This is a protected compound, but no place is too safe in the Philippines these days, especially here in Mindanao."

Cassandra had never felt that she was in any personal danger from the rebels. She had nothing they wanted—neither money nor arms. She agreed in theory with some of their causes, but she totally disagreed with their methods. Though changes were being made on the islands, they were not coming fast enough for the impatient malcontents who resorted to lawlessness to accomplish their purposes. Even Adam was not safe.

"Did you know the logger who was killed last year?" she asked. Aware that rebel threats had been part of the reason for moving away from the old site, Cassandra wasn't without fear for Adam's safety.

"I'd met him."

His terse answer was less than she'd hoped for. She wanted to be reassured that it wasn't possible for the same thing to happen to the man she was growing to love, but she knew there could be no such assurance in *their* world.

"Come on," he motioned, preceding her on the

59

path. "I've got that early-morning meeting." They were nearly at the house before he turned and spoke again. "Something's come up and I'm going to be staying here for a few days."

Despite her resolve, Adam's words were a disappointment to Cassandra. She had been looking forward to his company on the flight back. She had even hoped he would escort her to the mission compound personally. She wanted his company, even if she couldn't seek or accept his love.

"Business?" That was the logical answer, but somehow she felt there was more to his change of plans.

"Partly."

He offered no further explanation and she was left to speculate. An image of long black hair and darkly flashing eyes filled her mind as she entered the house and made her way to her room, causing her to wonder if Triana Valdez played any part in his sudden decision not to leave the next afternoon. Even if Cassandra couldn't have him, she knew Triana was wrong for Adam. She wanted what was right for all of them—even the beautiful, designing Triana Valdez!

CHAPTER 6

NEGLECTING HERSELF THESE PAST FEW DAYS had been a mistake. Loss of sleep, waning appetite, and overwork were taking their toll, Cassandra reasoned. She rarely napped after lunch, though she knew that, for many, the practice was routine during the heat of the day. Today was an exception. Wiping her forehead, she wondered if the temperature could really be as oppressive as she felt it to be. Cassandra shifted to her left side in another effort to find a comfortable position.

The night before had yielded little rest. Remembering how she had tossed and turned, Cassandra was surprised that Jodi had been undisturbed. More than once she had wanted to cry out to her teammate, but the pain in her right side had lessened by morning, and now the area was only mildly tender.

Accumulated exhaustion from the last three nights drew her willingly into the world of slumber. Gone, at least for the moment, were her worries about the mission's fate, the concern she was beginning to feel over the possibility that she might really be ill, and the nagging fear that she was in love with Adam Ralston, despite her best intentions. The only thing Cassandra felt was the weight of her body drifting down into the thick mattress. Like a small child resting in the arms of a loving mother, she felt secure and safe.

She slept through the afternoon and into the night, waking to find a watchful Jodi seated next to the bed. An oil lamp cast its shadows. The ethereal quality of the scene matching the muddled state of her mind. Cassandra felt certain the fever had returned, for the tablets she'd taken earlier would no longer be aiding her if indeed they had ever taken effect.

"Here," Jodi prompted, holding out medication and a glass of water. "Take this. . . . If that sets okay, I'll go make you a little soup." A look of concern crossed Jodi's face. "You've been awfully edgy since you returned from Butuan . . . this must have been coming on."

After a few swallows, Cassandra tried to hand the glass back. "Drink it all," she was ordered. "You don't want me to have to tell George when he calls in the morning that you haven't been obeying the doctor's orders. . . . He got back to Butuan this afternoon, and base said he had a dinner meeting with the hierarchy of Pacific Lumber."

Cassandra hoped the meeting meant good news. "What time is it?" she asked, stifling a yawn. Observing the pitch darkness outside her window, she knew it was late. "I must have slept for hours. I can't believe I missed the evening call."

"That was two hours ago."

"Two hours!" Her eyes darted to the watch still about her wrist. "It's after nine!" Swinging her legs over the side of the bed, Cassandra shakily rose to a standing position.

"And where do you think you're going?"

She had no energy to protest as Jodi lowered her

onto the bed. Cassandra's head was spinning. She couldn't remember ever feeling so miserable. During her past three years with the tribe, she had been very fortunate. Many of the workers who trained with her had suffered from amoebic dysentery, malaria, hepatitis, and even tuberculosis, but she hadn't contracted anything more serious than a slight cold . . . until this.

It's probably nothing, she assured herself, once more trying to stand. "I'd like to go to the bathroom," she smiled weakly at Jodi, who continued to block her way, "unless you're so set on keeping me here that you want to go to the clinic and get a bedpan."

"Well . . ." Jodi's expression told Cassandra she was seriously considering that option.

"Jodi Campbell . . . you wouldn't dare!"

"Testy, aren't we?" Moving aside, she allowed Cassandra to pass. "I always thought you'd make a lousy patient . . . the pill pushers and needle stabbers always do."

Cassandra walked as far as the door, where she paused for a moment and rested her weight against the wooden post. "A professional opinion, I presume."

Cassandra's jab recalled their standing good-natured banter about Jodi's need to be tutored through the mission's first-aid course. Jodi was a great linguist, but it was no secret that she had no interest or aptitude for medicine. "At least when I'm really sick I know the place to be is in bed," her maligned roommate retorted.

"Okay," Cassandra sighed, by now resigning herself to the fact she wasn't physically up to doing much else. "Let me get cleaned up and change into my gown, and then I'll climb back into bed."

Fishing under her pillow, Jodi pulled out the practical cotton garment and prepared to carry the lamp so they could see their way through the darkened house. "You'll probably be better by morning," she stated cheerfully.

"Sure," Cassandra laughed, clutching her side as a cramp ripped through her body.

"Hey! You okay?"

"I'm fine . . . it only hurts when I laugh." The pain was lessening already. "I think I may have pulled a muscle, or something."

"That wouldn't surprise me!" Jodi clucked. "The way you've been pushing yourself since you got back. . . . Anything happen at the party you haven't told me?"

"Nothing!" Cassandra knew her sharp reply had only raised Jodi's suspicions. "I just had to catch up on the time I missed." It was a flimsy excuse, but she couldn't admit even to Jodi that her mind had been filled with thoughts of Adam Ralston. Only work could drive his haunting image from her. It was her secret, and it would remain her secret. Not even to her dearest friend would she confess the dawning truth that she was falling in love with him. . . .

Morning did bring a modicum of renewed vigor, but there was no substantial improvement in Cassandra's appetite, even though she had not really eaten in over twenty-four hours. Actually food had little place in her thoughts as she waited for George's call.

Fighting between the government and the rebels still continued in the area originally slated by Pacific Lumber to be the next logging site. With only a few weeks of timber-cutting left at the old location, they'd be forced to move on or suffer a costly time lag. There was no guarantee that anything had been decided the night before, but the waiting had become interminable. Cassandra hoped to hear—one way or the other. Either way, her chances of seeing much of Adam in the future were almost nonexistent.

The familiar crackling of the radio set was reassuring as Jodi turned it on. It wasn't the best system of communication—what they were allowed to say on the air was limited, and privacy was nil. But the monitoring of other calls gave them a link with the outside world, and in times of trouble or disaster provided valuable information.

Cassandra sat beside Jodi as she gave her call letters and waited for their sked. She had hoped to get right to the results of the meeting, but she was forced to listen to the preliminaries before George finally introduced the subject.

"Met with the loggers," she heard George say. "Do you copy?"

"Roger, we copy." Cassandra knew that Jodi's use of the radio jargon was only a game they played. Though much of what was transmitted over the radio was in code, very little of it needed to be. "What's the score?"

"Loggers zero, mission three . . . we won!"

"Victory!" Jodi's shout would have awakened the tribe if they hadn't already been up and stirring. "Three . . . really?"

"Affirmative," came George's laughing answer.

The mike was thrust into Cassandra's hand before she had a chance to fully assimilate the meaning of his words. "Here!" Jodi instructed. "I have to tell Fely and the rest. We've been promised three more years!"

"Jodi . . . Jodi . . . You still there, C-29?"

"Affirmative, F-120 . . . Cassie here." She knew the code numbers, too, but since it was a favorite toy of Jodi's, Cassandra usually let her handle the calls. "We copy. . . . Great news!"

"You did it, baby!"

"*He* did it," Cassandra corrected, wondering what the others listening thought of George's familiar term. If Adam were monitoring, it would only confirm the

65

relationship she had allowed him to believe existed between herself and the mission base manager.

"*He* sure did," George laughed, "with a lot of help from one blue-eyed angel . . . Gotta sign off . . . angel."

There was much she wanted to say to this dear friend, much she needed to share, but being on the air wasn't like using a private telephone. Cassandra couldn't broadcast her dilemma, and George was the only one, besides her Lord, whom she knew would understand.

"We're remembering you." It was their traditional sign-off, and it meant they were praying for each other. But somehow today those words were not enough—she needed more.

We've won! Cassandra kept reminding herself, but she didn't feel like a winner. She had done what she had set out to do. The whole purpose of her meeting with Adam Ralston had been to save the tribal work. The work was secure for at least another three years. Jodi and the others hadn't come down off their cloud yet, and it had been almost three weeks since they had first heard the news. So why wasn't she jubilant, too?

Sighing, Cassandra shifted in the bed. An afternoon nap was now a necessary routine for her. The other symptoms had pretty much abated, but without a few hours' sleep in the middle of the day, she found herself too tired to function. She had begun to wonder, as she lay awake some days thinking of Adam, if the cause of her lethargy might not be psychosomatic. She knew it would be easier to recover from a physical illness than to forget the man she couldn't allow herself to love.

She hadn't heard from Adam Ralston since he said goodbye at the Butuan guest house. After their lunch he'd left for the plant, not even accompanying Cassandra to the airport. His pilot had seen to everything, even her escort back to the tribe. He was pleasant enough, but he wasn't Adam Ralston.

A commotion at the front door broke into Cassandra's thoughts as she lay trying to rally enough energy to get up after her short rest.

"It's Marta!" The frightened look on Jodi's face as she barged into the room told her all she needed to know.

"It can't be!" Cassandra shouted, jumping up and quickly slipping into her shoes.

"The labor has just started," Jodi informed her. "But I don't see any way she can hold out until we get transport. . . . Why did it have to be a month early?"

This couldn't be happening! Just last week Cassandra had finally persuaded Marta's husband Manggi to agree to have the baby delivered in a hospital.

The now inescapable fact that the fetus was in breech position had left him no choice, if he wanted his wife and child to survive. With Marta's history of miscarriage, Robert Howard, the young Australian doctor with the logging company, had warned her that she would most likely need a Caesarean section if she ever managed to make it to term.

It had been a difficult decision for the two young Christians. Marta's father was the village Datu, and it was Salvador himself who had predicted that his daughter would die in childbirth because she had forgotten the gods. Death was accepted in the tribe, but to die outside the tribe was a major taboo. Marta had taught Cassandra and Jodi the language and had learned to trust them as friends long before she'd trusted their God. Now her life and that of her unborn baby were in their hands.

Marta was not scheduled for admission to the hospital for two more weeks. It had seemed a good estimate of time, considering that this would be her first full-term delivery. Cassandra had never observed a Caesarean, and it wasn't the kind of surgery attempted by an amateur. Again, she found herself wishing she had far more training.

"We don't even talk to base for another four hours," she sighed, wishing she had known of Marta's condition a little earlier. "They couldn't possibly be here until morning . . . and we can't wait until then."

"What can we do?"

"There's a doctor at the logging camp!" Cassandra remembered Adam's less-than-glowing reports of Dr. Baker, but said nothing. "If we get there and he's away, maybe I can convince Adam to have his pilot fly us out—if there's still time. . . . Either way, we have to go down the trail."

It wasn't a foolproof plan, but they knew if they didn't act quickly, they would lose two lives. Cassandra couldn't bear the thought of such a tragedy. Marta was one of their closest native friends. In addition, her father wouldn't hesitate to use his own daughter's death to point out the missionaries' ineptitude and the impotence of their God. She had to try!

The threatening sky told Cassandra they could be in for some rain. "Get someone to hitch up a carabao and stretcher. We need to leave as soon as possible. If this storm hits, the going will be rougher, and we won't have as much daylight left. . . . Oh, and see if you can get a couple of volunteers to come with us in case we run into anything unexpected."

They'd had very little trouble with rebels, but they'd also made it a point not to be on the trails at night. Cassandra wasn't really worried, but it was wise to take a few extra hands along as a safety precaution. The stretcher could fall apart, or the carabao go lame, and then there would only be Manggi and herself to carry Marta.

"It'll have to be some of the strong believers," Jodi warned. "None of the others would want to defy Salvador."

It was true. Old superstitions died hard.

"I'm going to Marta." Cassandra knew that the young girl would be frantic. "Tell Fely that we need her help. The men won't question her word. I just hope Manggi doesn't let us down and refuse to let her go."

Both women knew that if Manggi said no, Marta would obey. She would stay in her little hut and die. Even if Marta made the trip, she might still die. Wearily Cassandra bowed her head and prayed that God would provide a doctor at the base and that all would go well.

"You sure you're up to this?" Jodi's concern was sincere and appropriate. "You have been ill . . . maybe I could go. . . ."

The thought of Jodi on a medical mission brought a smile to Cassandra's lips, despite the seriousness of the situation. "Thanks . . . frankly I'd rather not be going, but if everything else failed, I could at least try for a normal delivery."

"I know," Jodi sighed. "Manggi has heard of my handiwork and wouldn't let me within ten miles of his wife. Dr. Kildare, I'm not."

"Unfortunately, neither am I."

"Well . . . God provided a lamb for Abraham; maybe he'll provide a doctor for us." Jodi's optimism was real. One didn't undertake their kind of work without believing in miracles.

A drenching rain had fallen upon them for twenty minutes, and there was nothing left to keep dry. Cassandra tried to protect Marta with a plastic sheet, but the wind blew it back each time, leaving the girl cold and shaking. Her contractions were closer together and more intense now, and Cassandra could only hope the birth could be delayed as long as it took to get her to a doctor.

"Breathe!" she coached her friend, pushing back the wet strands of dark hair plastered to Marta's face.

"You're doing fine. . . . We shouldn't be much longer."

Normally they could see the end of the trail by now, but the going had been slow, impeded by the weather. Never could Cassandra recall the journey being so interminable.

With the latest contraction over, she tucked the sheet about Marta once more, hoping to shield her from at least some of the gusting wind and rain. "Why is rain always cold, even in a tropical climate?" Cassandra groaned in her own tongue. She knew that none of her companions understood her words, let alone the scientific reason behind their uncomfortable state.

The dark clouds were robbing them of the little light that was left of the day. Cassandra had watched the clouds tumble overhead, knowing they could only spell trouble. The rain had started with a light sprinkle, but not much time passed before the sky opened up to turn the firm path into a bog. Her once-blue sneakers were covered with mud, the soil marks on her jeans creeping up another inch with each hole she stepped into. Her concern was for Marta, but now her own strength was flagging, and Cassandra found herself praying that she would not have to be added to the narrow stretcher that lumbered behind the faithful carabao.

With a near drought in the area, the Christian farmers had been praying for rain, but Cassandra couldn't help wishing that the Lord had said "Wait" this time. Lush green vegetation would greet them on their return, but as she felt the mud oozing through her toes, Cassandra's thoughts were not of the future.

In this kind of weather, she knew the logging company wouldn't be likely to risk its plane or pilot to save a native. From what Adam had said about Dr. Baker, he might even refuse to help them anyway. And if he did refuse, she would undoubtedly be bringing back bodies for burial instead of a new life. They needed that miracle.

It wasn't Cassandra, but Marta's husband who first heard the sound of a truck engine over the steady pounding of the rain. "Logger!" he shouted, rushing ahead of the group.

The two other men swatted the rear flanks of the plodding animal in an effort to speed its pace. Though the tired beast protested, it obliged. Another contraction claimed Marta as she fought to stay atop the bumpy bed. Her hands gripped the edges, knuckles white from the strain.

"We're going to make it!" Cassandra encouraged, knowing that Marta's reserve was waning. "Just a few more minutes and we just might have our miracle!" she assured her in her own tongue, shouting above the din.

The compound was only a short drive from the place where the trail joined the road, but it was a long walk for all of them in their drenched and exhausted condition. Given the late hour and inclement weather, Cassandra doubted there would be other transport if they missed this one.

Manggi's excited voice cut through the air, telling them that he had been able to stop the vehicle.

"Thank God!" Cassandra sighed in grateful relief, the slush no longer bothering her as she pushed through the downpour. "We've made it!"

A taller man followed behind Marta's husband, and Cassandra sensed, even before she could see clearly, that it was Adam Ralston. Silently she prayed. She didn't want to feel any troublesome emotion when she looked into Adam's eyes. She didn't want to feel anything. Cassandra watched as his long stride put him well ahead of Manggi. The khaki shorts and shirt were plastered to Adam's well-formed body, his rain-soaked hair appearing darker than she remembered. When he drew near, she could see that his jaw was set

71

in anger, and those clear blue eyes that she remembered so well were narrowing with each step.

"Cassandra Wellsley. . . ." He was close enough that there was no need for his shouting. Grabbing her by the arm, he forced her to one side of the trail. "You idiot! Couldn't you tell that it was going to storm before you started out on this blasted trip . . . I gave you credit for some sense, but I can see that I was wrong!"

"Adam—"

"If I hadn't been called out on an emergency *and* just happened to see your man waving frantically when I chanced to look in my rearview mirror, you'd *still* be out in this torrent."

"I *am* still out in this torrent!" Cassandra cried, pushing back the wet clump of hair that had fallen across her face. "You haven't really solved any of our problems yet . . . have you, Mr. Ralston?"

"Come on!" he snapped, propelling her toward the mouth of the trail. "We'll settle this later."

"No!" Pulling away from him, Cassandra ran over to the carabao and began to prod the beast. "We have to get Marta to your doctor!"

For the first time Adam noticed the stretcher behind the animal. He watched as another contraction began. "What's wrong with her?" Motioning for Cassandra to stop, Adam knelt beside the woman, felt her forehead, and sought Marta's wrist for a pulse.

"She's not sick!" Cassandra's impatient tone reflected the exasperation she was feeling. "Can't you tell that Marta is having a baby!"

"A baby!" Straightening up, Adam took in the rain-drenched form. "You mean to say that you dragged this poor woman all this way through the jungle in the worst rainstorm we've had in months—and the sole purpose was to have her baby delivered by a doctor?"

"Yes—"

"Then you're a bigger idiot than I thought! Surely

72

by now you know that the tribals don't use doctors to deliver their young."

Adam's choice of words was degrading, making her beloved people sound like some kind of livestock. "Marta—"

"Have you timed the pains?"

"Yes . . . no . . . ," Cassandra faltered, "not in the last few minutes." Adam Ralston had a disturbing knack for causing her to feel like the idiot he was calling her.

"Doctor?" At the sound of Manggi's voice, Cassandra was aware for the first time that the three natives were observing their heated exchange with increasing concern. "Marta? . . . Baby? . . ."

"Let's get her to base. We'll have to deliver!" Without looking back, Adam turned briskly and marched off in the direction from which he'd just come.

"Wait!" Cassandra called after him, rushing to catch up. "Marta has to have a doctor!"

Braking suddenly, Adam whirled to face Cassandra, nearly sending her sprawling into a nearby mud puddle. "And where did you expect to find one of those? Behind a coconut tree?"

Cassandra felt too desperate to appreciate Adam's sarcasm. "Not that you'd care . . . but if we can't get your Dr. Baker to do the delivery, they'll probably both die!"

Placing his hands squarely on her shoulders, Adam peered into Cassandra's troubled face. "Die?" he questioned. "Why do *you* believe they'll die?"

Near tears, Cassandra hurriedly explained the baby's breech position and the Australian doctor's prognosis. "Will Dr. Baker help? He's Marta's only hope!" As she spoke she saw Adam's expression change to one of grim concern.

"He can't do a Caesarean—"

"But surely—" Cassandra protested. It may have

73

been years since the older man had been called to perform a section, but she knew that he had certainly been trained in the procedure.

"He can't!" Adam's words were emphatic, almost angry.

"Talk to him . . . tell him . . ." Cassandra pleaded, her eyes moving helplessly to the approaching party—first to her friend Marta, and then to Marta's young husband who had dared to defy his powerful father-in-law in order to give his wife and child a chance at survival. They had trusted Cassandra, and they had trusted their new-found God. "He *has* to help! . . . Remind Dr. Baker of his Hippocratic oath . . . anything!"

It couldn't end like this! Marta was a Christian, but Cassandra wasn't convinced that it was her time to be called home. There had to be some way to reason with this man who still had the nerve to call himself a doctor. She would talk to him herself if Adam refused.

A sudden gust of wind whistled through the glistening palms like the cold finger of death, molding the thin fabric of Cassandra's cotton blouse to her slender form. She felt disembodied, as if it were all a dream and she, only an onlooker. Her fatigue was playing tricks on her mind, she reasoned. She would have to keep fighting to focus all her energies on the problem at hand.

Adam's mood was thoughtful and he made no further move to propel them toward the waiting truck. His gaze was fixed on Marta and Manggi. Cassandra wished that he really knew them—if they were his friends she knew that he would not rest until Dr. Baker agreed to do the section.

"Maybe if I talk to him—" Cassandra suggested when Adam remained silent.

"You can't. . . . He's not here!"

Simple words, simply stated. Cold, hard facts.

"When will he return?"

"He won't."

"He won't?" Did he really speak those words, or was it just her subconscious giving voice to the worst of her fears?

"He . . . won't?"

"No."

There was no need to remain victim to the elements. Accepting Adam's lead, Cassandra walked beside him willingly to the truck. The men helped Marta into the jeep, the youngest volunteering to follow on foot with the carabao. Manggi sat beside his wife, comforting her with each new and closer contraction. Cassandra was too weary to think as they drove to the compound. There was no real hurry now, for when they got there—there would be no real help.

Adam was silent as well on the trip to the base. Most of his attention was directed to maneuvering the muddy trail, but not even Cassandra suspected the great inner battle that was raging. By the time they reached the house, he would have to decide on a course that could change his life forever.

The engine had only just been shut off when Adam turned to Cassandra. "Dr. Baker can't do this C-section."

"I know!" Cassandra countered, irritated by his need to remind her of the hopelessness of their situation.

"But what you don't know—is that I *can!*"

CHAPTER 7

THE LIGHT WAS FADING from the near-evening sky, but Cassandra could clearly make out the simple Western design of the field guest house. It wasn't as elaborate as the one in Butuan, but it was a welcome haven from the storm. A power generator provided the compound with electricity, and she knew they would surely have running water, though possibly not heat.

A trail of mud and moisture followed them as they were herded through the once immaculate entrance and on to the clinic where Marta and Manggi's child would soon be born. It was all happening too quickly for Cassandra to comprehend. Her Lord had answered their prayer for a doctor in the most surprising manner imaginable.

There had been hints, she realized now. She had suspected that Adam had received more medical training than the average manager, but she had been unprepared to learn that he had completed med school and was only four months from finishing up his internship when he dropped out. He'd offered no explanation, only warning her that it had been ten years since he had practiced medicine.

Remembering that he had mentioned not having seen his daughter in the same length of time, Cassandra wondered if Adam's wife had been the one to walk out on the marriage. Maybe she had taken the child and Adam didn't know where either of them was living. Something as traumatic as that experience might explain why a man could turn his back on so much training. Medicine wasn't the kind of thing one normally just walked away from without a *very* good reason.

"Where is that boiled water?" he demanded. Adam had been barking orders since they'd hit the door. "Cassandra, go see what's keeping my housegirl." Cassandra hesitated, watching as Adam and Manggi placed Marta on the table. "Are you going to go, or do I have to do it myself?"

She knew that the poor girl hadn't had enough time yet, but she decided that it would be better to obey than to argue with Adam in his present state. "Yes, doctor!" For her words she was rewarded first with a steely look, and then a reluctant smile.

"Sorry." His expression softened, and Cassandra knew tension was responsible for the edge in his voice. "They say it's like riding a bike—you never forget. But if they're wrong, it won't be my knee that gets skinned this time."

Cassandra wanted to hug him to her, like a mother comforting a small boy afraid of the dark. Adam Ralston was scared. He desired to do his best for Marta, but Cassandra knew that there was more to it than that. Adam feared the past. It wasn't only his rusty medical skills that he doubted. What he doubted most was his ability to face up to, and conquer, whatever it was that had so devastated his life ten years before. He was hurting, but she could only help if he would let her.

Crossing the room, Cassandra took his hands in hers. Gazing up into Adam's eyes, she knew that all she felt for him was there in her own eyes for him to see. "You'll do fine. . . . I know you will."

Squeezing her hands, Adam lowered his face to Cassandra's and placed a breath of a kiss on her waiting lips. "You . . . my dear . . . could inspire a man to do *anything*."

A moan from the table brought them back to the task at hand. "The water," Cassandra reminded Adam, edging away from him. "I'll go check."

She needed to escape, if only for a minute. Adam had said she could inspire him to do anything, but Cassandra knew Adam Ralston was no one's pawn. He had built the walls around his heart, and he would have to be the one to knock them down. As strong as their mutual attraction was, Cassandra knew that, even for her, he would never pretend to be what he wasn't—and for that she was grateful.

The infant was reluctant to leave the warm shelter of her mother's womb. In protest, she screamed her dissatisfaction to the world. Assisting in the birth had been something that Cassandra would not soon forget. Adam had been wonderful! Even given the limits of facility and time, Cassandra couldn't have asked for anyone better. His skilled hands were meant to bring healing; of that she was certain. How he could have ever left his calling was still a mystery.

The light meal Adam had asked her to make was almost ready. After dismissing the housegirl for the night, he had stayed to put the instruments away properly and see that mother and child were settled in. Cassandra was looking forward to some time alone with Adam. He had said they needed to talk—and it was true. She knew so little about him, when she wanted to know *everything*.

She had just finished transferring the contents of a saucepan to a warmed plate when Adam came up behind her. "Hmm . . . smells good."

"It's nothing. . . ." Cassandra dismissed, fishing in the drawer to find something with which to serve the fried rice. "I just threw a few of your leftovers together."

"I didn't mean the food." Turning her to face him, Adam held Cassandra close. "I can see you sneaked a shower and begged some of my housegirl's clothes." Holding her from him, he smiled that beloved crooked smile. "I can't ever recall this looking as good on her."

It was only since meeting Adam that Cassandra could remember blushing so much. His close scrutiny made her vastly uncomfortable. Cassandra was taller by several inches than the Filipino girl whose *mahlong* she had borrowed. When Adam's eyes trailed to the garment's hem and the expanse of tanned leg now visible, she could feel her color rising considerably. "Let's eat before it gets cold," she said, flustered.

Her attempt to disengage herself was futile. Instead of releasing Cassandra, Adam slowly bent his head to hers. She sensed that this would not be a sisterly kiss like the one she'd received earlier. The seconds of waiting gave her both time to consider turning away and time to anticipate the fulfillment she craved. Instead of resisting she lifted her lips to meet his.

This had been a day crammed with emotion. In the jungle Cassandra had felt exhausted and afraid. In the clinic she had shared in the apprehension and joy of saving a friend's life and bringing a new one into the world. Now, in Adam Ralston's arms, she felt safe and protected. Tomorrow was soon enough to face the reality of their relationship. For now, all she

80

wanted was to savor the sweetness of his mouth on hers, to be glad that she was a woman.

Gone were all the past suspicions and pain. Banished were any thoughts of future regrets. The clean scent of Adam filled her nostrils, her subconscious registering the fact that he, too, had showered after officiating at the birth. The cologne he'd chosen was intoxicating, and she reeled dizzily in his arms.

For the first time in her twenty-seven years, Cassandra knew what it was to need a man's love. She knew all the rules, believed in all the rules, but, until now, it had been such an easy game that she'd never considered cheating.

"Adam, I—" she mumbled against his mouth.

"Tell me that you love me, Cassandra," demanded Adam. "These past three weeks have been torture . . . knowing that it was George Sanders and not me on your mind."

Cassandra couldn't admit the depths of her feelings for Adam, for then there would be no escape. Yet things had gone too far for her to fall back on George as an excuse to keep them apart. She knew Adam wouldn't believe that deception after the way she had just responded to him.

"I . . . I don't love George," she admitted reluctantly. "At least not in the way you mean." Biting down on her lip, Cassandra turned away from Adam and he let her go.

Picking up the plate, she set the rice on the table and then went back for the rest of the meal. "George and I have always been close . . . but I could never . . . never—"

"Marry him," Adam finished for her, his expression changing as if he'd just remembered something. "Yes, you would definitely be the marrying kind. . . . One couldn't expect a missionary to do anything else, right?" Though his words were mocking, his tone was not. "As a group you are all so—so controlled. Why is that? Is your faith really that strong . . . or is it that you don't have emotions like the rest of us?"

Cassandra had no appetite for the food she had just dished out for herself. Those emotions that Adam evidently thought her incapable of had been pushed to the limit. How could he say such things after the last few minutes? Was he angry with her because she wouldn't say that she loved him? Was his bitterness against God so complete that he saw her as a trophy— a way of getting back at the God he felt had betrayed him in some way?

For a moment she had seen Adam as kind and caring. Had Adam felt she coerced him to save the lives of Marta and her child and that now she owed him something? He seemed to want her to fall in love with him, but at times Cassandra doubted that his reasons had anything to do with genuine caring.

White-faced, she breathed back the tears that were fast forming. Without a word, Cassandra marched from the kitchen and down the hall to the room she had been shown by the housegirl. Once inside, she threw herself onto the bed and allowed the floodgate to break. There was no way things could ever be right between herself and Adam. If she had needed proof, he had certainly supplied it for her that night.

When Marta and the baby were strong enough to travel, they would leave. Any further business between the mission and the logging company would have to be handled by someone else. If she never had to speak to Mr. Adam Ralston again, it would suit her just fine!

Burrowing even further into the soft mattress, Cassandra refused to be awakened. It couldn't be morning, her numbed mind reasoned; it felt as if she'd only just slipped into bed. "Go away. . . ." she moaned, pulling the thin covering up over her head. The action did little to block out the light or the annoying sound of rattling china.

With eyes tightly closed, Cassandra sensed rather than saw the intruder continue the advance into the room. The housegirl was only following orders, but she wished that the young Filipina would be remiss in her duties for once. Not even the tantalizing aroma of freshly brewed coffee could tempt Cassandra from her warm nest.

Silence prevailed in the modestly decorated room and the rhythm of Cassandra's breathing slowed as the admiring intruder looked on. Shifting in her innocence, Cassandra tucked the edge of the cover beneath her chin and cuddled the length of the pillow against her. A smile of contentment stole across her face as she settled down in peaceful slumber. Like a glittering Christmas tree shrouded in a cloud of angel hair, Cassandra's muted loveliness shone through the protective mosquito netting.

Adam's eyes savored her serenity, wondering how he could have said such callous things to her the night before. She was more beautiful each time he looked at her. Quietly he unfastened the wisp of material that separated them and reached down to caress Cassandra's soft cheek.

She stirred and nuzzled the hand, dreaming of Adam. This Adam Ralston shared her goals, her faith, and her love. He was her knight in shining armor, and together they braved the world as one, but it was all only a wonderful dream!

Adam moved closer, bumping against the bed.

"Adam!" she gasped. "What? . . . How? . . ."

Her heart was pounding uncontrollably, and she knew that only a small portion of her reaction was attributable to the shock he had given her. He was too close to allow her to function normally. And to her amazement, she now realized that despite everything, even last night, the attraction for him remained strong.

Tearing her eyes away from his, she noticed the tray and realized that it had been Adam, and not the housegirl who had awakened her. Her muffled mind was finally beginning to accept the shapes of day.

Pulling the netting away from the side of the bed, Adam gave a tight little chuckle. "It's time you got up, love."

Registering his words, Cassandra forced herself to a sitting position. "I . . . ah . . ." she fumbled, her censoring scowl only serving as fuel for Adam's enjoyment. "How long have you been in my room?"

With the lifting of one eyebrow and a corner of his mouth, he looked the rake. Smiling broadly, Adam clicked his tongue and shook his head. "Afraid the mission wouldn't approve?"

"It's not that," she objected. However, Adam's words caused her to consider for a moment how his presence in her room might appear to others.

He planted a playful kiss on Cassandra's pursed lips before backing away. "Actually you could tell them that mine was an errand of mercy. I brought your breakfast. And I promise our little secret will be safe with me—providing you eat everything."

Adam's eyes were twinkling and Cassandra regarded him closely. In this mood it was hard not to like him. Last night she had thought him capable of doing her harm to feed his own ego. This morning, she felt certain she'd been mistaken. He was an angry man, but an honorable one.

"Is it a deal?" he persisted.

Cassandra wasn't the type to enjoy conceding a battle easily. Her fingers toyed with the pillow beside her, tempted to throw it at Adam. With her luck, however, she would come out the worse for the exchange.

"Trying to blackmail me?"

"No," Adam countered, covering the short distance between them and taking the pillow from her as if perceiving her thoughts. "My mama taught me never to tangle with skinny women—especially those armed with deadly weapons."

Placing the pillow on a nearby chair, Adam continued. "Now be a good girl and eat your meal before it gets cold."

Skinny! Cassandra knew she had dropped a few pounds in recent weeks, but she would hardly consider herself skinny.

"Hand me the tray . . . and then you can leave." Given a few more "compliments" like that one, she would be tempted to throw more than a pillow.

"Not so fast!" Adam set the tray before her and pulled up a chair for himself. "I'm not so easy to get rid of."

"So I've noticed."

" . . . and I'm not so sure you really want me to go."

Cassandra tried not to look into Adam's eyes, but when she did, their eyes met and she couldn't deny the truth of what he had said. She *didn't* want him to leave. She wondered about this man, remembering that first day when, for a fleeting moment, he had delighted in the words of a children's Sunday school song and then abruptly retreated into his shell. Had he once possessed a faith as deep as her own, or had he been like so many others—just empty words? Was Adam running from God, or had he never really found Him?

A heavy silence filled the room as Cassandra picked at the lovely breakfast. Again this morning she had no appetite. It had been days since she'd eaten a full

85

meal. The very thought made her ill. "I'm sorry . . . It's really nice, but . . ."

Studying her closely, Adam took in the pallor of her skin. "You don't look good—"

"Thanks!" Cassandra snapped. She knew she must be a sight in the crumpled *mahlong*, her hair uncombed.

Ignoring her wounded vanity, Adam came nearer. "I didn't notice it before, but your color is off. . . . It could just be a touch of the flu, but it could be . . ." Removing the tray, Adam examined Cassandra's eyes. "Have you been tired lately?"

"Yes . . . but we've had a busy schedule."

"Hmm . . . How long has your appetite been off?"

"Adam—" she protested, not enjoying the role of patient.

"Any fever?"

"Just because I didn't eat your breakfast is no reason for you to diagnose me as terminally ill!"

"Your fault," he laughed, retreating for the moment. "You pressed me into service after all these years."

"How are Marta and the baby?" He hadn't mentioned them yet, and Cassandra was eager to know that they were doing well.

Walking over to the open window, Adam peered out across the compound. The activities of the day had started hours ago. Equipment was being moved to its assigned locations, and his men were working at the site and down at the log pond. Adam liked his job; it had filled his days and occupied his mind, but it had never brought him the peace he had hoped to find. And lately, he found his mind constantly filled with thoughts of Cassandra. She challenged the safe little world he'd built around himself, and he knew he'd never be content with it again.

"Anything wrong?" Cassandra's anxious voice broke into Adam's pondering.

"No." His tone was reassuring, and Cassandra knew that his furrowed brow wasn't due to any problem with her friend or the child that had just been born to her. "I peeked in on them before I brought your food." He gestured toward the unfinished breakfast. "Seeing their baby reminded me of the first time I saw my little girl. . . . Jenny was so tiny."

Cassandra stiffened as she watched Adam close his eyes in remembrance. The pain was there in the tight set jaw and the heavy sigh that was released before his eyes reopened. "She'd be in junior high now . . . probably looking exactly like her mother did at that age. The baby pictures were identical . . . Sue always thought she looked like me around the eyes, but I could never see it. A towheaded angel . . . I miss them."

Cassandra didn't know what to say. She'd never been a parent or a marriage partner. She'd been trained to counsel others, but she felt too close to this, and, to her surprise, even slightly jealous of the love that Adam obviously still felt for his former wife. Undying love for the child she had expected, but she'd never thought that he would still care for the mother—not after so many years. So the break-up *had* been her decision.

Pulling a chair over, Adam sat quietly, his eyes appraising Cassandra. "Sue was a lot like you." Shifting, he trailed his gaze down her long honeyed hair, pausing at her unsmiling lips. "Not in appearance. . . . She wore her hair short, and it was several shades lighter. Her eyes were blue, but pale like mine. . . . Ten years is a long time, but I haven't forgotten any of the details."

Cassandra swallowed, her throat dry and tight from the strain. Why was he doing this? She knew she should be glad he was opening up. Adam needed to dispel the ghosts and face the past, but didn't he know how hard it was for her to listen? She had confronted him with his calling as a doctor, and he had delivered Marta's baby. She supposed she owed him this much.

Adam spoke almost as if Cassandra were not there, lost in his own world. "My cousin introduced us. Sue was a pretty little thing in her nursing whites . . . it was she who sparked my interest in medicine. I was into forestry and had thought of veterinary science . . . but my plans hadn't progressed any further." The sound of a Jeep driving past caused Adam to pause and glance in the direction of the window. "On sunny days like this, I'd go over to the hospital where she was training and we'd share a sandwich from the local deli. There was a grassy area with this one huge shade tree—that was our favorite spot. . . . They expanded the parking lot a few years ago, and I hear that whole area is gone. . . . It seems everything we had together is gone now."

Rising from the chair, Adam took Cassandra's hands in his and sat back on the edge of the bed. "Sue had faith like you. She believed in the goodness of God. . . . She even had me convinced of it for a while."

Was Adam saying that his wife was a Christian? Had his bitterness toward God sent her away? Was he telling her this because he now realized he wanted his family back? Though she could feel the battle raging inside Adam, she knew that he had still not come to terms with God.

"Do you know where she is?" Cassandra asked, not sure that she wanted to hear the answer. "Is your daughter with her?"

His laugh was bitter. "Yeah . . . I know where they are." The pressure he was exerting on Cassandra's hand increased as he spoke. "I was in the last months

of my internship when I lost them . . . or should I say
. . . God took his own?''

Adam's wife and daughter—dead? Cassandra's
face turned white. ''How?'' she gasped, fighting back
the tears.

''Does it matter?'' His words were tinged with
anger. ''After Sue and Jenny were killed, I got a lot of
empty platitudes . . . especially from the 'Christians'
around me. Some just didn't know what to say.
Others didn't even try. They gave me a lot of 'pie in
the sky' but nothing of substance.''

''You can't judge God by people.''

''I didn't,'' Adam argued. ''They just confirmed my
findings.''

''Do you really believe that?'' Cassandra didn't
know if she were weeping for his loss, or because he
was so full of bitterness. As long as he blamed God,
he would never heal.

Releasing her hand, Adam drew her to him, placing
a tender kiss on her forehead. ''Hey . . . it all
happened a long time ago.'' Reaching into his back
pocket, he withdrew a handkerchief and handed it to
Cassandra. ''I didn't tell you to upset you . . . I just
felt it was wrong letting you go on believing—whatever it was you were believing. At first I used it as a
wedge to keep us apart, but now—well, I would
rather there not be any more wedges.''

Drying her tears, Cassandra looked up at Adam,
wishing it could be so easy.

''I never wanted to hurt you.'' As he softly traced
the curve of her jaw with one finger, Cassandra knew
that he meant every word. ''You're the best thing that
has happened to me in ten years.''

''Adam . . . I . . .'' she protested, as he wove his
fingers through her hair and brought his lips to bear
briefly on hers.

Almost reverently, Adam placed his hands on either

side of her face, forcing her to look up at him. "I wanted to tell you last night," he whispered huskily. "Instead, I stupidly started condemning you for something you could never have had a part in . . . I was arguing a case that I knew was lost . . . the evidence was against me, but I had to make a final plea." His eyes impelled her to listen. "I can't make any promises. Knowing you has caused me to doubt some of my long-held conclusions. I once said that you weren't any different from those pious hypocrites I once knew . . . but you are! You're so real, Cassandra. It's not so much what you say or do—it's what you are."

"Don't, Adam . . ." Wrenching her face from his hands, Cassandra turned on her side, refusing to look at him. "Don't put me on a pedestal . . . I might fall. We all do from time to time," she sighed. She felt tired and drained, no longer able to to deal with her mounting fatigue. "Don't judge God by people, Adam—good or bad. Your faith has to be your own, or it's no faith at all."

"And without faith there is nothing," he misquoted, causing Cassandra to look at him in surprise.

"Yes," she sighed heavily. "And without faith there is nothing."

CHAPTER 8

MARTA WAS EAGER TO GET BACK to the tribe and show off her firstborn, but Adam insisted she wait until the incision was well on its way to being healed. Marta wasn't accustomed to being pampered, but Cassandra felt she secretly enjoyed it, despite her protests to the contrary. The housegirls did all the work, so there was really very little for the two women to do, except visit and watch the baby grow stronger each day.

It was Cassandra herself who wasn't growing any stronger. It had been five days since her walk through the storm, but her energy had not returned. With Adam away much of the time, she had been able to rest for hours without his knowledge, but it was getting harder to hide the persistent pain in her right side. If he'd noticed, he hadn't said anything, but she had felt his watchful eyes on her on more than one occasion.

"She's beautiful," Cassandra beamed, bending down to play with the tiny fingers of her namesake. "Your father is not going to be too happy with the name." She directed the comment to Marta who shrugged away the objection.

"He is a stubborn man," Marta agreed, gently rocking the makeshift cradle. "But maybe baby Cassandra can fall between the cracks of his pride. His heart is not so hard as it used to be. He has not believed . . . but he has seen."

Cassandra's thoughts were of another stubborn man. Adam had made no further mention of his family, or the issue of his faith since that first morning. The subject seemed closed. Though she longed to be in his arms, Cassandra was thankful for this new distance that Adam had chosen to put between them. She loved him for his understanding, but her heart ached for a deeper unity between them. She couldn't give herself without giving her faith, and she couldn't allow him to take only half of her.

"Someday . . ." Marta smiled, looking first at her daughter, and then at her friend, "when you marry, you will make pretty babies."

The thought made Cassandra blush. In one of her dreams there had been children—hers and Adam's.

"You do know how to make babies, don't you?" Marta laughed, such discussions common in her society. "Or does Dr. Adam need to tell you how?"

It wasn't until Marta's eyes traveled to the doorway that Cassandra straightened to see who had entered the room. She felt certain that Adam couldn't have missed Marta's last comment, as it had been intentionally directed at him.

His knowing smile infuriated her. "That's the best your color has been since your arrival," he stated on a half-serious note. "Am I to understand that you are in need of a doctor?"

"No!" Cassandra shouted, glaring crossly at both of them. "I'm not seventeen!"

"Seventeen?" Adam laughed. "In this day I doubt

many make it to the age of ten without knowing—or at least thinking they know—as much about sex as their parents."

The wails of a crying infant pierced the room. "Now see what you've done!" Cassandra scolded, reaching into the cradle to remove the little one. "Shhh . . . Shhh . . ." she crooned, gently rocking the unhappy child. "Aunty Cassandra's here. . . . Shhh. . . ."

The newborn quieted momentarily, routing up against Cassandra's breast.

"I don't think it's Aunty Cassandra she wants," Adam laughed.

"Here," Cassandra conceded, placing the fretful child in her mother's arms. Marta received her willingly and, without motioning for either to leave the room, began nursing her hungry baby.

Cassandra watched the happy pair, doubting if she would ever experience the wonder of motherhood. She had always wanted children, but with her heart so bound to the man now standing beside her, she wasn't sure she would ever be free again. She couldn't marry Adam, expecting him to change. She could patiently wait, hope, and pray, but she wouldn't compromise her position. To marry a man who didn't share her goals would be unfair to both of them. The Bible spoke of not being unequally yoked, and Cassandra knew that it meant even more than the Christianity of both partners, it meant that they were both to pull in the same direction through the power of Christ.

Arm around her waist, Adam was pulling her out into the twilight of evening. There was no formal garden like the first time in Butuan, but the smell of jasmine twining around the rear doorpost brought back the memories. During that stroll, she had been dressed in jeans, too, all the finery of the party discarded.

The party had raised many questions about Adam, but none of them seemed to matter now. It had been weeks since she had even thought about the beautiful Triana. The threat to her happiness was not another woman, but something much less tangible. A flesh-and-blood opponent would be less formidable than the enemies of the spirit that kept the man she loved locked inside himself. He was afraid to trust, afraid to open his heart and believe.

Keeping in step with the man beside her, Cassandra knew this Adam was no illusion. Her fanciful mind had stopped reaching for the unreal; it was now trying to grasp and deal with the reality. Dreams had waltzed Cassandra into this love that tore at her heart, but to continue in them would only whisk her into ultimate destruction. Cassandra Wellsley had to be strong, or cease to be. It wasn't physical death she feared, but the death of her inner self. She knew that thousands committed this suicide everyday, but Cassandra had fought for all she'd valued for twenty-seven years, and she wasn't ready to retreat now.

Millie and George had supported her choice of profession, but it hadn't been easy to stand up against her parents' apathy, her friends' amazement, and her Aunt Ernestine's all-out war. Her single status, coupled with her good looks, had even caused problems during mission training. By the time she reached the field, dealing with jealous wives and skeptical instructors had become routine. She had proven herself, and now at conference time they all laughed over her battle stories, but none of it had been funny during the process. God had seen her through this far, and she knew He wouldn't desert her now.

Silently Cassandra accepted Adam's lead and walked with him to the only bench that the compound boasted. The leaves of a small bauhinia fluttered above them, resembling a horde of large green moths

94

as they labored in the gentle breeze, getting nowhere. The tree's orchidlike flowers sat regally atop their individual perches, accepting the homage of the curious double lobes, as if it were their due. No one questioned their right to center stage. It was as natural as nature itself.

The sounds of the tropical night were beginning. It was these voices that Cassandra had listened to for the last three years and called "friend." The whine of the generator, and the hum of distant conversations were the strangers. Stars as familiar as family blinked their 'hello,' the ever-changing moon adding the only contrast. Clear skies played host to the mounting splendor, the clouds that had escorted them to the base having blown on to haunt another people.

Fighting the urge to lean back against Adam's broad chest, Cassandra held herself rigid. She knew that the tenuous control of the last few days had to be maintained if she were to have victory over the countless days to come. Her energies had to be spent on reality, not wasted on fantasy.

Manggi and the men had already returned to the tribe, and in a short time Cassandra would bring his wife and new baby back to him. It would be easier when she was physically separated from the temptation of seeing Adam each day. Like a dieter in a candy store, or an alcoholic in a bar, her willpower was weakest when the object of her desire was nearest.

As if reading her thoughts, Adam stood, raking rough fingers through his coarse, graying hair. The familiar gesture struck a chord in Cassandra, her sharp intake of breath dispelling what was left of the carefully monitored façade of composure. Lazily his gaze compelled her, the liquid blue of his eyes rushing through her like fiery lava upon the waiting land. There was no hesitation in her taking his outstretched hand.

"Let's walk," he whispered.

The barren trek of land boasted no beauty as they strolled along the dusty trails. Hints of the past could be seen in a stray tree or an isolated patch of grassy vegetation. The frantic movement of men and machinery had all but blotted out the wilderness of the valley, replacing it with functional starkness. Cassandra missed her jungle.

Family huts dotted the perimeter of the compound. She watched as the flickering of distant lanterns fought against the encroaching night. Her families back in the tribe would be preparing for evening, too. Cassandra wished that she were with them now. It was much too dangerous walking beside Adam in the moonlight.

"Marta and the baby are doing well," Adam pronounced, breaking both their stride and the tense silence. "She should be ready to leave soon." Taking Cassandra's other hand in his own, Adam forced her eyes to his. "I'll miss you."

Cassandra was already feeling the loss, imagining the long days without sight or sound of Adam. "I . . . I'll miss you, too." She hadn't wanted that catch to be there in her voice, but it was.

A warm breeze whisked by, setting aloft the loosened tendrils of Cassandra's tightly bound hair. The clip's inability to adequately control her thick tresses mirrored Cassandra's frustration at her own lack of discipline over her riotous emotions. Something akin to fear filled her eyes as Adam lazily sought to release the artificial restraint of her hair.

A sign of exasperation sped past Adam's open mouth as he saw her silent plea. He withdrew his hand. "Is this game really necessary?"

"What game?" Cassandra knew that Adam could only be referring to their enforced distance and the false denial of an attraction that neither really wanted to fight. "This isn't a game, Adam."

"I know." There was no rancor in his voice, but Cassandra watched his taut jaw, knowing he was holding himself in check. "I should hate you for what you are doing to my life . . . but I can't. You and I aren't as different as you might think . . . but we aren't as much alike as you need."

"As we both need," Cassandra corrected, finding the strength to stand her ground. "I don't know where your faith lies, Adam. You won't let me get inside your mind—you won't let anyone, not even God."

Turning from her, Adam gazed out into the night. "You don't understand. For ten years I've been putting brick on mortar. You don't just lay that kind of spiritual wall to rubble by one sweep of the wrecking ball. I'm no Joshua. *He* had God on *his* side and he still had to march around the city of Jericho seven times."

Cassandra remembered the story well. "But God's on *your* side, too," she assured him. "You have to believe that."

Adam's eyes were expressionless as he allowed them to meet and search Cassandra's. "Maybe when I believe *that*, I can believe the rest."

Adam's words haunted Cassandra as she prayed her way through the days. In the morning she would be leaving with Marta and the baby. Cassandra knew that she should be sleeping instead of stealing around in the base kitchen in the middle of the night, but she was restless. Her side ached, and she could find no position that was comfortable enough to allow her to drift off to sleep. Even the preparing of her tea had seemed a major effort, and she wondered how she was going to make it on the long walk back to the tribe.

Like a hawk, Adam had watched her during dinner. Cassandra knew that it was stupid to try to hide her illness from him, especially now that it was clear the problem wasn't going to disappear on its own. But she didn't want to delay her return or to spend more time in his company. The last week had stretched her to the limit. Adam had constantly asked how she was feeling, and Cassandra wasn't sure that he'd been satisfied with her answers. Thankfully, after tomorrow she would be beyond his watchful gaze.

It hadn't all been bad, Cassandra told herself, stirring at the already dissolved sugar in her cup. Marta and the baby were alive because of this trip, and her presence had at least caused Adam to think more about his faith. She knew now that he was a doctor, and that he hadn't divorced his wife or deserted his child, but somehow all that knowledge made it even harder for her to resist her love for him. Before, she hadn't understood. Now, she did. Understanding hadn't changed anything. The facts were still the same. Adam Ralston and Cassandra Wellsley lived in two different worlds, operated under two different value systems. As long as that remained true, it was wrong for her to entertain any thoughts of a future together.

Finishing her tea, Cassandra rinsed the cup in the sink and set it on the sideboard to drain. The sound of little Cassandra's crying alerted her to the lateness of the hour. At next feeding it would be time for them to wake and prepare for the journey home. If she was lucky, she might get four hours' rest.

The persistent pain was getting worse instead of better. Gripping the counter, Cassandra held her breath, waiting. It seemed always to be there now, not only when she overexerted herself. The slightest movement triggered enough discomfort that she could no longer ignore it.

"Cassandra?" The tentative question originated from the shadowy doorway.

She pretended not to hear as she stood with her back to Adam.

"You okay?" he persisted, striding purposefully toward her. "Couldn't you sleep, either?" Adam's voice was thick with emotion as he misinterpreted the cause of her insomnia. "I kept thinking of your leaving in the morning."

It was a dark night, and the one small light that Cassandra had switched on did little to illuminate their surroundings. Adam made no effort to improve the dimly lit conditions as he came to place his hands on Cassandra's shoulders. A bigger-than-life silhouette cast against the wall alerted her to his intent even before the nerves of her body signaled the reality of his touch.

Gently his fingers kneaded the tight muscles, working their way up to the smooth column of her neck and back down again. Cassandra could feel herself relax as the pain left and the warm sensation of his ministrations filled her being.

"Better?" Adam whispered turning her to face him.

The thin cotton *mahlong* Cassandra had continued using as a nightgown offered scant protection against the warmth of his touch. Like ice in summer she melted into his broad chest, not caring for the moment what others might think.

"Adam," she sighed, as the bristles of his day-old beard played along the line of her jaw.

"Must you leave?" he coaxed, tightening his arms about her.

Her quick intake of breath caused him to close his arms even tighter, misinterpreting her accompanying whimper.

"Cassandra, what's wrong?" he demanded, at the next unmistakable cry of pain.

99

Clutching her right side, Cassandra silently pled for understanding as Adam peeled back her fingers and gently probed the localized tenderness. Gasping with each new stabbing pain, Cassandra's eyes filled with tears, but even through the watery curtain Adam could see that she had allowed her condition to progress beyond reason. A pale yellow tinge replaced the normal brightness of her eyes, and he knew that he couldn't let her return to her duties with the tribe in the morning.

"Try to get some rest," Adam sighed, his voice evidencing his concern and exasperation. "I'll have to make some arrangements."

"Adam—" His name trailed from her lips as she placed a hand on his retreating shoulder. "I'm sorry."

"Sorry!" he blasted, his controlled anger bursting forth. "What were you going to do if I didn't notice? . . . I suspected that you had a mild case. I asked you enough times how you felt, but I could never get a straight answer out of you." Running a hand through his hair, Adam paced the floor. "I didn't know about the swelling."

"I thought I was getting better," Cassandra argued.

"Do you call being doubled over at the kitchen sink at two o'clock in the morning *better*?" His eyes raked over her like she was a child who hadn't the sense to come in from the rain. "I wrongfully called you a fool when I found you on the trail a week ago, but *then* you had a good reason for endangering your life. What's your excuse for this one?"

Cassandra hadn't considered that she might be endangering her life, although she was well aware that the outcome of hepatitis could be death when there were serious complications. Rest was the usual prescribed cure, but rest hadn't been enough for her and she had known it for days. Now the possibility that she might have done some permanent damage was very real. She had heard of an occasional case developing into cirrhosis, or even hepatic coma, but it seldom happened in someone as young as she.

"Is it really necessary that I go into the hospital?" Adam's steely expression told her the answer even before her words were out.

"If you're thinking of backing out—forget it. I have business in Manila anyway, so you aren't even taking me away from my work."

"Manila!" she cried. "Why not Butuan or Davao?" Cassandra knew that the Mindanao hospitals were primitive by comparison, but she hated to be so far away.

Adam was not inclined to argue. Placing an arm around Cassandra's shoulders he propelled her toward her room. "Let's just say that I don't want to share your visiting hours with George Sanders."

Adam hadn't given her anything for the pain, saying it would mask the symptoms, but somehow Cassandra managed a few hours of sleep. She wondered, as the housegirl awakened her, if Adam had even seen the inside of his room that night. She seriously doubted it. There would have been the plane to be fueled, the pilot to be alerted, and the hospital to be notified.

Slipping into her freshly laundered jeans, Cassandra pondered how long she would have to stay in Manila. The recuperation period could be lengthy, and Cassandra hoped Adam wasn't under any illusion that she was going to spend all that time away from her people. She could rest in the jungle as easily as in the city, she reasoned, knowing full well she had never *rested* in either place. It wasn't her nature to be idle. That was going to be the hardest part of all—especially since the enforced bedrest would give her time to think and daydream.

Thinking and daydreaming had become dangerous

pursuits of late. Once they had been a coveted part of her days, but that was before she'd met Adam Ralston—the focal point of all her imaginings. The problem was not that she disliked thinking of Adam. The problem was that she liked it too much.

The sun wasn't even up, Cassandra noted, as she cast a glance out the window, but it would be by the time they taxied down the runway, and Marta and her escort started their journey down the trail. She wished she could go with them and see Datu Salvador's face when he first laid eyes on his daughter and new grandchild. Cassandra hoped that he would lay aside his false pride at least long enough to rejoice that they hadn't died as he'd predicted, but she feared that he would be just as stubborn as ever.

The knock came sooner than expected. Pushing the borrowed brush through her hair, Cassandra placed it on the nightstand and went to answer the door, her impatient caller rapping once more. "Just a minute!"

At five-seven, Cassandra had never thought of herself as short, although many of her friends during her modeling days had towered above her. She remembered trying to use her little more than average height as an argument against even starting in the business, but her determined aunt had given her objections only cursory consideration. It was the stony expression of the man standing in the hall that now made her wish for greater stature.

"The pilot's ready," he announced stiffly. "How's the pain?" Cassandra wondered if Adam's inquiry was born of friendship, or simply the concern of a doctor for his patient. He seemed so controlled, as if during the long hours of the night, his anger had magnified.

"Not bad," Cassandra answered truthfully. "Maybe I'm on the mend." Her last words were hopeful, but Adam's censoring glare told her that he

102

didn't accept her mild improvement as reason to call off their trip to the hospital.

"Marta's waiting to see you."

It was a dismissal of the subject. Cassandra smiled her reluctant acceptance, following Adam to the kitchen. With two groups readying for departure, the room was crowded. Little Cassandra, strapped to her mother's back, slept contentedly amidst the confusion. Canteens were filled, and the last of the breakfasts were scraped from plates, signaling that if Adam's men were to avoid being caught by the heat of the sun, it was time for those taking the trail to leave. The waning darkness was deceptive, the benevolent-looking ball of fire creeping upward, somewhere just above the treeline.

"I have to stay," Cassandra explained as she approached her friend, unsure if Adam had told Marta that she would not be returning with her.

"I'm glad," Marta confirmed to Cassandra's surprise. "It is right that you stay with Dr. Adam."

There seemed a hidden meaning behind her words. Had Marta sensed the attraction between them, or was she only referring to the wisdom of Cassandra's receiving proper medical attention? "Tell Jodi not to try and do it all while I'm away . . . I won't be gone long."

Cassandra's last words brought a narrowing to Adam's eyes. A look of understanding passed between the native woman and himself. "Tell Jodi that Cassandra will return when she is strong enough and not before. . . . The settlement isn't under enemy occupation, and she's *not* McArthur."

Cassandra opened her mouth to argue, but decided against it. She and Adam would be spending the next few hours in close quarters as they flew first to Cebu, and then on to Manila after refueling. Adam hadn't the power to make her stay against her will, and she

103

knew that it would be several days yet before she would have to fight that battle. At the moment they were both exhausted and they were not alone. It was neither the time nor the place for a declaration of war.

"I will tell her," Marta agreed obediently, her eyes darting from one to the other. "She will be happy . . . she has been worried about Cassandra."

"And why's that?" Adam's tone was casual enough, but Cassandra bristled under his intense glare. "Hadn't she been well *before* the trip out?"

Shifting nervously from one foot to the other, Marta smiled tightly, realizing that her words had added to the already tense atmosphere. "She would be well now if it hadn't been for me . . . and my baby." The guilt in her expression told Cassandra that Marta believed what she was saying.

"No," Cassandra comforted, gently touching Marta's arm. "It isn't your fault."

The exhaustion suffered on the trip could have contributed to the progression of the illness, but her stubborn refusal to acknowledge her symptoms had been equally to blame. "There was no other way," she reasoned, her eyes pleading for Adam's acceptance. "I would have gotten ulcers if Jodi had taken you and I had had to sit back and wait to hear the results. . . . Anyway," she smiled, caressing the cheek of the sleeping infant, "is this the face of a Jodi?"

CHAPTER 9

IN THE ISOLATION GOWN AND MASK Adam looked every inch the doctor, Cassandra decided as she sat back against the plumped pillows, smiling as he entered her room. Tomorrow they would be moving her into a regular room, if today's tests confirmed the ones from the day before. Cassandra wasn't overly concerned about being contagious, but hospitals had stringent rules about such things. The people with whom she came in contact were far more likely to contract hepatitis from their own exposure to its primal causes than from her. In the large cities sanitation wasn't all it should be; in the back country, it was practically nonexistent.

She had taken the usual precautions. Even so, health hazards came with the job, and she had known all along she would have to accept the dangers. In her five years in the Philippines, this was her first real rub with what some of her co-workers had been battling almost from the time they'd set foot on foreign soil.

Why God worked that way, she didn't know. It

seemed that it was often the most dedicated who were weeded out. Cassandra didn't know their hearts—only God knew—but she doubted the premise held by some that it was a test of the faithful. The hardships of the field would, and did, discourage the faint-hearted and marginally committed, but they weren't the only ones forced to leave. Cassandra knew if her illness didn't abate, she, too, would be among the casualties.

"Hey . . . why the long face?"

"Nothing," she dismissed, chiding herself for her pessimism. The worst possible outcome was that the mission would insist she take her overdue furlough. "I guess I was just feeling sorry for myself. I'm not an indoor person, and I detest hospitals!"

"And the people who make you go there?" Adam questioned. Cassandra could see the twinkle in his eyes and could only guess that, beneath the mask, his mouth was turned up in that familiar grin. "Have you forgiven me yet?"

Giving him her best smile, Cassandra nodded. It wasn't a matter of forgiveness; it was she who had acted like a spoiled child. She'd wanted God to just make it all go away—the illness as well as her love for Adam. When all the circumstances of her life remained unchanged, she knew she'd just have to accept His timing.

Adam said nothing as he scanned the stark room. The pale green of the walls, the mechanical bed, the utilitarian chair were not unlike those in any big city hospital. "A touch of home . . ." he laughed, sliding the chair closer. "My wife used to accuse me of living at the hospital and just dropping in at our apartment when the mood hit me." Taking a seat, he gave Cassandra's hand a companionable squeeze before continuing. "I was so dedicated to my cause then . . . I never saw the truth of what she'd said."

Cassandra found herself wanting to hear more

about Adam's marriage. Sue Ralston was gone, but she felt a strange kinship with this woman who had died even before Cassandra graduated from high school. They had loved the same man, and may have even shared the same faith. Sue, of course, had married Adam, had borne his child. It was unlikely that Cassandra's love for him would ever find such fulfillment.

"Jenny was usually asleep by the time I got home . . ." Adam was saying, "but I did try to make it up to her on my day off." A faraway look invaded Adam's eyes. "At least that's what I told myself."

"I'm sure you were a wonderful husband and father," Cassandra assured him, knowing that it was futile to dwell on a past that couldn't be changed.

Adam's eyes probed Cassandra's face, as if by peering into her soul he could better see his own. "I wanted to be, and I would have been, if it hadn't been for my obsession to be, the very best doctor in my field. I didn't stop with school and the hospital. If there was a guest lecturer, or a specialist making rounds with another team—I was always there."

The kind of dedication that Adam was speaking of was something Cassandra had seen often among members of her own profession. So many viewed the ministry as a call to reach out exclusively to other people, often neglecting their own families, or feeling guilty on the rare occasions when they did spend time at home. It wasn't a problem that existed only in the secular world.

"We have that same occupational hazard in my line of work." Cassandra didn't smile. Bitter kids, broken marriages, and ruined ministries was not a trivial matter. "My pastor at home always took vacations each year, went away on the weekend of his wedding anniversary, and set one day a week aside for his wife and kids. It had to be a life-or-death emergency before he would change that date with his family, and when he did, he always tried to schedule another." Clearing her throat, Cassandra gave Adam a tight smile, remembering her attitude. "He took one afternoon for himself, even went to the club and played golf with my father sometimes—I didn't approve."

"Sounds like he was a real advocate of moderation," Adam chuckled.

"No," Cassandra disagreed. "Not exactly moderation, though I guess in the end it came down to that. It was really more a matter of priorities." Looking down at her hands, Cassandra dug her unpolished nails into her softly veined skin, wondering how to explain the difference to Adam. "People sometimes use the term *well-rounded* to avoid commitment. Pastor Williams was certainly well-rounded, though at the time I called it other things."

"Lazy . . . undedicated . . . worldly," Adam supplied.

"And worse!" Cassandra laughed. "He knew something then that I'm still not sure I've fully learned. We work so hard at not being conformed to the world's mold, and then willingly pour ourselves into the mold of other Christians. We get so caught up in doing God's work that we frequently lose sight of doing it His way."

It was a strange conversation for her to be having with Adam. Usually at the first mention of family and God, he changed the subject. Not today. Today he had been the one to bring it up. Adam had even talked a little about his medical training. It seemed so natural a discussion that Cassandra had no compunction about continuing as long as Adam would allow. His thoughtful silence caused her to wonder if that limit had been reached.

Before she could ponder further, the door to the room suddenly swung wide and both their gazes shifted to the young woman entering. A broad smile of greeting stretched across Cassandra's features as she watched the girl go about her work. Slipping a thermometer into Cassandra's mouth, the petite Filipina nodded her apology for the interruption. After taking Cassandra's pulse, she waited for the other reading before jotting both findings on the clip chart at the foot of the bed. Efficiently she checked the I.V., then turned to leave on rubber-soled shoes.

Waiting as the door crept to a close, Cassandra listened for the heavy click, signaling that it had reunited with the jamb. For long moments neither Adam nor Cassandra spoke, though they both knew that the nurse would by now be far down the hall and well out of hearing range. It felt eerie in the silent room. From the hallway, only the faint sounds of hospital equipment being moved from one location to another and an occasional muted voice could be heard.

For the second time in as many minutes the long hand of the wall clock moved, a jarring motion that challenged the onlooker to disregard the passing of time. There was an odd tension in the near silence, like the watching of clouds as they gathered for a storm. Cassandra wished that she could see Adam's entire face. Reading another's thoughts was never easy, but with the mask in place, his expression was inscrutable.

Suddenly Adam's gaze moved past her to the clock on the wall. "Sorry this has to be so short," he said, rising abruptly to his feet. "I promised Carlos Valdez that I would go over some figures with him tonight before we turned in." His brows shot up in a gesture of apology, but Cassandra doubted Adam's excuse.

"It's early," she complained. "Visiting hours have just started."

"I was here this morning," he reminded her, " . . . and last night."

"I know," she conceded, aware that Adam owed her no time at all. "I just get lonely."

Beneath the mask Adam gave her an understanding smile, but Cassandra couldn't see it. He was an expert on loneliness. Adam thought that after all these years he'd gotten used to it, but since meeting Cassandra he'd felt more alone than ever. She was everything he didn't want, but knew he needed. Cassandra's lifestyle and values didn't fit in with the Adam Ralston who stood before her; such a woman belonged in the life of the one who had died along with his wife and daughter ten years ago.

Looking back was like seeing a shadow of himself. A part of him still remembered fondly the purposeful young man he had been. A part of him still held to the old beliefs and fought to resurrect the Adam of the past. The battle had always been there, even before Cassandra had entered his life, but what had been only a border skirmish was now escalating into full-scale war.

"Adam . . . ," Cassandra ventured. His expression was so far away, making her wonder what turn his thoughts were taking.

Instead of answering, Adam's eyes drifted to the one small window in the room. All day clear skies had graced the heavens, fluffy white pillows of softness inching by against a backdrop of blue. Night was well on its way now, claiming the fleeting beauty of day and replacing it with its own version of loveliness. Like so many things that changed only to remain the same, Adam questioned whether a return to his faith would be lasting. Could he really live in close fellowship with God for a lifetime, or would the next crisis send him running again? Did he really desire to try again, he wondered, or was his growing love for

Cassandra the major motivation? He knew that his answers could only be found in the doing, but he was fearful of taking that first step.

"I must be going," he blurted, suddenly needing distance between them. "I may stop by in the morning, if there is time after the meeting ... tomorrow night for certain. Triana will be with me."

"Triana?" Cassandra exclaimed, the mention of the girl's name an annoying reminder that Adam was staying in the Valdez home. He hadn't spoken of Triana, so she had foolishly assumed that the designing female was away somewhere. "You're bringing her here?" Cassandra's tone was harsher than she had intended it to be.

"Actually I'm taking her to a party ... and she's been concerned and asking about you, so I thought we'd just leave a few minutes early so she could visit with you, too." Walking as far as the door, Adam's eyes narrowed once more. "The kid's having a hard time accepting her stepmother, especially with the news that Margarita is expecting a baby. Having someone like you as a friend would be good for her."

Cassandra hadn't been aware of the fact that Carlos Valdez's wife was pregnant, but the news didn't surprise her. She knew Valdez would be disappointed if she failed to produce a male heir, and, if the woman succeeded, it could only increase the animosity that her stepdaughter already felt toward her. Triana Valdez was too selfish to see the new baby as anything other than a threat to her own position. Furthermore, Cassandra doubted that Triana wanted a friend anymore than she wanted a sibling or a mother.

Adam's eyes were compelling, asking her to understand and to help, but she couldn't. She wasn't physically or emotionally competent just now to handle the volatile young beauty, she excused herself.

111

Adam apparently didn't know the Triana Valdez she had met that night at the party. Triana had declared war and Adam didn't even know that he was the disputed property. The girl was coming to spy on the enemy, not to lay down arms.

"When is the baby due?" Cassandra couldn't see Triana as the doting big sister, but she prayed that she would at least show enough maturity to limit her fight to those able to fight back. "How do you think she'll react?"

Adam paused. "She's been an only child for so long. . . ."

"She's *not* a child! Triana is twenty-two years old!"

Silently Adam calculated the years since his arrival in the Philippines. "Hmmm, I guess you're right. I still see her as that skinny seventeen-year-old who used to follow me around."

Cassandra found it hard to imagine the well-endowed young woman in that light. And Triana would be appalled to know that the man she imagined herself in love with still saw her as an awkward teen.

Cassandra herself had been a mature beauty by the time she was seventeen, but she remembered all too well that fragile stage of life. Her own trials had come, and continued to come, more *because* of her good looks, but Cassandra had never envied those on the other side of the fence, especially during those trying years when peers could be so cruel. The girls she'd envied were the merely attractive ones—neither loved nor hated because of their outward appearance. They weren't limited or pushed. They were free to be what they wanted to be, or so it had seemed to her then.

Her cousin, Melinda Powers, had been one of those attractive young women whose bright and bouyant personality made her an instant favorite with boys and girls alike. She was model quality—the wholesome, girl-next-door variety. So much to live for. So much promise. . . . But death had claimed her beloved Melinda at seventeen, just when the girl's whole life was opening up to her—and before she was prepared to meet eternity. Cassandra could have helped, but she had never found an opportunity to share her faith with Melinda. She was so young and there would be time for that—later. . . .

It was for all the Melindas of the world that Cassandra had become a missionary. But it was her guilt over failing the most important one that had delayed her mission training. Instead, right after graduating from high school, Cassandra had become the model Ernestine Powers wanted—in the stead of her only daughter.

Now Cassandra faced another challenge. To her utter dismay, she realized she wasn't seeing Triana Valdez through the eyes of a loving God, but through the brilliant blue of a jealous Cassandra Wellsley. She found it easier to love the foul-smelling, betel nut-chewing women of the tribe than the perfumed, fastidiously dressed young woman. But though Triana did nothing to stir her sympathies, Cassandra's Christian commitment demanded that she love—even her enemies—and at this moment, Triana Valdez offered the greatest threat to her happiness.

"You don't like Triana, do you?" Adam asked, his question remarkably perceptive. "I thought you missionaries were supposed to love everyone."

Cassandra's throat constricted with the pain of his words. Because of her lack of charity toward Triana, she was failing Adam. But hadn't she warned him not to put her on a pedestal? "Adam, I . . ."

"No," he expelled his breath in a long sigh. "I'm sorry . . . I had no right to condemn you." Moving the isolation gown aside, Adam placed his hands into his pants pockets and shifted his weight from one foot to the other. "Considering how rude she was to you at the party, you've been very civil. . . . I just hoped—"

"You noticed!" Cassandra's eyes went wide with surprise.

"I'm not blind," he laughed, strolling back toward the bed, his urgent need to depart forgotten. "We men see a lot more than you women give us credit for, but we're also smart enough to know when to keep our mouths shut." Taking her hand in his, Adam softly traced little circles atop the ridges of Cassandra's veins with the tip of his thumb, the intimate gesture noticeably relaxing her features. "Triana is used to being the center of attraction . . . I think she would have approved of Jonathan's missionary, but you, my dear, spelled competition."

"Then you know about the designs Triana has on you?"

"Me?" Adam's laugh was hearty as he released Cassandra's hand and clapped his own together. "You're a charm, Cassandra! Triana sees me in the same light as you do George Sanders."

"No," she protested. "She told me—"

"What? To keep away from me?"

Cassandra's nod was decisive.

"The little rascal . . . I know," he corrected, seeing Cassandra's look of disapproval, "Triana is no longer a child. Yet emotionally she has never grown up. She wants to keep all those she cares about to herself— for fear of losing them."

Adam's reasoning might be accurate to a point; she really didn't know Triana well enough to judge. But she knew when another woman wanted more than friendship from a man.

"Did she tell you she intends to marry me?" The lines of Adam's eyes crinkled in a smile. "That's what she told me when she left for college."

"But she's serious!" Cassandra warned, her frustration mounting.

"Sure she is . . . as serious as the little girl who wants to marry her daddy, or the boy who sees himself walking down the aisle with his beautiful science teacher." Sitting on the edge of her bed, he again took Cassandra's hand. "When the right man comes along, Triana will forget her little fantasy. I've tried telling her that, but now the pretense seems more important than ever. It started when I first came. Her mother had just left and gone back to Spain."

"For a visit?" Cassandra asked, knowing that it was unlikely.

"No, she had left Carlos for good."

"Without Triana?"

"Without Triana," he confirmed. "Carlos Valdez can be a hard man. Mrs. Valdez waited until Triana was nearly grown before leaving Carlos. He wouldn't give her the freedom she asked for and her child, too. He wouldn't even allow his ex-wife to stay in the same country with her."

"Did Triana know?"

"She knew . . . and she blamed her mother for leaving, and her father for not making her stay. She was very confused, but proud even then. She loved them both, and for a time hated them both." Adam watched as Cassandra's expression softened. "I was still licking my wounds. I guess in many ways I still am. Triana and I made a good pair—I needed someone to care for, and she needed security . . . I thought I was helping, but sometimes I wonder. Since I was twice her age, I never dreamed she would think of me as anything but a friend. I was floored by her announcement at first, but after a while I began to see it for what it was. She'll get over me."

"Is that what you want?" She had to know his

115

answer. "Do you want her to get over you? Most men would find it flattering to be desired by a wealthy, beautiful young woman."

"Why, Cassandra Wellsley! If I didn't know better, I'd say you were jealous!"

"Don't be silly!" Snatching her hand away, Cassandra sat up poker straight. "I just don't want anyone to take advantage of you."

"Triana?" he laughed. "Or you?"

Swallowing, Cassandra pushed back against the pillow, the hole she was digging for herself growing deeper with each word. "I don't care what you do, but if you really care for Triana, like you say, you won't encourage her. If she's transferred her affections to you because she hates her parents—"

"Did I say that?"

"You said—"

"I said for a time," he corrected. "Actually they get on rather well. She only hates her stepparents now."

"Mrs. Valdez remarried?"

"Certainly. That's why she finally divorced Carlos."

"Oh," Cassandra emitted a small sound.

"She never loved Carlos Valdez. It was an arranged marriage, and when the wife of her true love died, she left Carlos, or so the story goes." The eyes above the mask twinkled with mischief.

Cassandra had never understood the practice of arranged marriages. It all seemed so cruel, though she knew that it was still an accepted practice in some cultures. Money and position were often greater inducements than love, even in her own civilized world.

"Would you ever marry someone you didn't love?" She couldn't resist asking the question.

"You mean, would I ever marry Triana Valdez so

116

that some day I could be president of Pacific Lumber. . . . You really ought to say what you mean, Cassandra." His tone was indulgent. "Or are you asking if I would marry her for her firm young body, and that flowing dark hair, like raven's wings, and her skin soft as doves? . . . Is that what you're asking?"

"No," Cassandra groaned, turning her face from his. "I thought you said you thought of her as a child!"

"It was *you* who pointed out that Triana had become a woman," he gently reminded, forcing her to look at him. "Wasn't it?"

Closing her eyes tightly, Cassandra bit down hard on her bottom lip. Slowly she opened her lids to find an unobstructed smile on Adam's lips. The top ribbons of his mask were untied and now it lay inverted against his ample chest.

"I think whatever I'm likely to catch from you I've already got, don't you?" His piercing blue eyes lazily surveyed her, his lone finger rising to trace her jawline, then purposely moving to tease the lines of her mouth. "I admire you, Miss Cassandra Wellsley. You get to me in a way that a hundred Triana Valdezes never could."

His look hypnotized her, causing her words of resistance to flee from her thoughts.

"I think I like you best when you let that halo of yours slip a little. It makes you human, and allows a guy like me to hope that he might even have a chance of making it into that guarded heart of yours. . . . You make me want to revive the old Adam Ralston, while at the same time tempting me to cheat and just pretend that I already am. But that wouldn't work," he sighed. "You know the real thing too well to accept a fake."

Her puzzled expression made him smile. "It makes sense, even if you don't understand. Winners never

117

quit and quitters never win. What do cheaters do? Do they win the game and lose the pennant? Baseball never was my game." His eyes left her for a minute, only to return and devour every feature, like a man hungering for what he knew he could never have. "But then you wouldn't know—you don't play games."

There was an edge to his final words, confusing her further.

"You asked me if I would ever marry someone I didn't love. It's a fair question," he continued, "but I won't answer it. I think you know the answer as well as I know that you wouldn't marry someone just because you *did* love him." Standing, he put several feet between them before retying the mask. "I know I'm a puzzle to you, but lately I'm a puzzle to myself." He was out the door without even a goodbye, the heavy divider lumbering to a close, framing Adam's exiting figure.

It was a strange exchange, but one that Cassandra thought she was beginning to understand. He had opened up to her that evening, but nothing was settled, least of all in the mind of Adam Ralston. He needed time to sort through things, and as hard as it was for Cassandra to grant him that, it was the only way. His self-examination would determine their future. If he failed to reach the right conclusions, they would have no future together.

The darkness outside was complete now, as Cassandra strained to see any life beyond her window. The sound of rain against the windowpane made her spirits droop, the memory of the earlier sunlight forgotten. Picking up the glossy magazine that Adam had brought her that morning, Cassandra leafed through the pages, looking at the pictures. The image of a model she hadn't seen in years jumped out from one of the ads. She wondered if her former coworker had ever tried the shampoo she was so eagerly endorsing. Closing the magazine, Cassandra returned it to the portable tray that stood to one side of her bed. She didn't feel like reading.

Adam had spoken of cheating, of pretending. But he wasn't any more a fake than she was, and Cassandra knew it. The kind of love they both wanted would have to be based on truth if it were to stand the test of time. Pretense and cheating could have no part in it; the fires of living always burned away the deceptions eventually.

Switching off the light, Cassandra leaned back against the pillow, hoping for a few hours sleep before the next round of nurses and medication. The tapping of the rain had diminished, and she doubted that there would be any evidence of it when the morning sun rose to greet her. She listened as its soothing sound lulled her into God's natural interlude of slumber.

CHAPTER 10

CASSANDRA EXPERIENCED A STRANGE EMPATHY with Pavlov's dogs as she waited for the familiar clanging of the meal cart to stop outside her room. Her present semi-solid fare more closely resembled the famed scientist's canine offerings than she cared to think about. Cassandra wasn't even particularly hungry, but in the day's boring routine, mealtime was a welcome diversion.

She had been moved out of isolation shortly after lunch, but as the stripped bed on the other side of the curtain was still unoccupied, Cassandra hadn't noticed the difference. There had been no calls or visitors, making her wonder if Adam and Triana would show up for the evening hours. Forced solitude was new to her, and Cassandra liked it even less than she'd anticipated. It gave her too much time to think.

The sound was getting closer. Cassandra shifted in the rock-hard bed, wedging a pillow behind her back so that she could be more comfortable as she ate.

Impatiently she waited, the renewed clanging signalling that she was next.

"Good evening," the plump female aide greeted from the door, in her stilted English. "Enjoy your dinner." Placing Cassandra's tray on the table, the woman turned and left the room.

Absently Cassandra chuckled to herself as she began uncovering the dishes. She wondered in how many languages the aide could recite these few lines, and if she ever got mixed up on which meal she was serving, or to which nationality. As Cassandra surveyed what she was expected to eat, she fervently wished that she might exchange with someone who was on a regular diet. It was better than her fare the day before, but still a far cry from anything she'd serve a fellow human being.

Cassandra could only pick at the dismal meal. If her intake were being monitored, she would surely get a lecture from the doctor in the morning. He had already made quite clear his opinion of her ignoring the symptoms of her illness for so long. She had felt like a little girl being scolded by her father for playing with matches, and she didn't like being relegated to that position.

If her own father were here, Cassandra knew that he wouldn't explode as his sister Ernestine was prone to do, his carefully worded disapproval always yielding him the results he wanted. Seldom did he ever give advice to his children, even when it was asked for, making the times he did all the more effective.

Her father would probably know of her illness by now, for after talking with Jodi, George would have wired her folks. In a few days Cassandra fully expected to receive a letter urging her to return home. Ever since Millie's death, her mother's correspondence had been peppered with concern for her health. Articles clipped from the newspaper, and bulletins from the World Health Organization often accompanied the missives with the latest church gossip and the antics of her brother's children. A trip home might be nice, but Cassandra couldn't see herself leaving the tribe—not now.

Mitch and Michael had both become fathers in the same year, and Cassandra had not yet met either of her nieces. According to their Great-Aunt Ernestine, the two toddlers were natural models. And from their pictures, Cassandra had to agree that Katie and Nelda were beautiful children. Predictably Aunt Ernestine had already mapped out the girls' careers, but her residence in Philadelphia, many miles away, precluded the possibility that she would be available to shepherd the babies through diaper and baby food ads.

Cassandra felt sorry for her aunt, but refused to plead a case with her brothers that she could not endorse. Work was everything to Ernestine, becoming all-consuming since the death of her daughter. With the opening of her own modeling agency three years ago, she had thrown herself into the business to the exclusion of all else—including her husband and son. Not even the birth of her grandsons had influenced her to deviate from her self-appointed goal of self-destruction, Cassandra thought.

In her last letter her aunt had mentioned the possibility of a photographic layout in the Pacific for one of her clients. The Philippines was the major contender for the site. If she did come, Ernestine Powers had already informed Cassandra that her time would be limited, not allowing her the 'luxury' of visiting the mission compound. She did, however, insist upon seeing Cassandra. She would expect to be met at the airport.

It occurred to Cassandra that her mail was being held in Butuan, and no one would open it, of course, unless instructed. Perhaps Aunt Ernestine was on her way now! If so, she would need to know as soon as possible. In the morning she would call headquarters there in Manila and have them inquire about her correspondence.

The visit wasn't likely to be a pleasant one, but if it took place while she was still in the hospital, Ernestine would use Cassandra's present condition to insist that her niece return to the States and to modeling. Such a likely scenario caused Cassandra to push the plate away with a wry look.

When the aide came to remove the tray, Cassandra could tell from the shake of her head that she didn't believe her patient had made much of an effort. Cassandra smiled sweetly and watched as the woman waddled from the room, shoving the half-eaten meal into an empty slot and determinedly pushing the cart ahead of her. Given her size, Cassandra doubted that she could possibly understand another's lack of appetite.

Weight had never been a problem for Cassandra. She hadn't dieted since her modeling days, and even then it never consisted of much more than limiting her sugar and practicing moderation. At least Aunt Ernestine couldn't complain that her favorite niece had gotten fat, Cassandra thought ruefully. Actually, her bout with hepatitis had caused her to drop too many pounds.

Glancing down at the ugly hospital gown, she was hardly reassured. With Triana and Adam due shortly, and the threat of her aunt popping in, Cassandra fervently wished that she had a more presentable nightdress and a modicum of make-up at her disposal. The best she could do with the standard kit that had been given her was to wash up and run a comb through her hair.

Struggling with the lines of the portable I.V.,

Cassandra valiantly fought to keep her backside covered while pushing the unwieldy contraption over to the sink area. With one hand tightly clasped behind her, Cassandra cleansed her face and then awkwardly oversqueezed the foul-tasting generic brand toothpaste onto the hard-bristled brush.

"Yuk!" The gritty, soda-based concoction was worse than the food.

It wasn't the first time she had tried the product, but there was no getting used to it. The foaming agent enveloped her mouth instantly. With eyes wide, she gave the mirror a clenched-tooth smile, holding up the brush in mock imitation of an ad for which she had once posed. As if on cue, a large glob of white lather oozed out one side of Cassandra's parted lips. In a rush to stay the flow, she quickly closed her mouth and jabbed at the creeping mass with her only free hand. The feel of the rough bristles as they tracked their way down the inside of her gown alerted her to the fact that the brush had escaped, its progress stopping at the waist, Cassandra's body taut against the counter.

"Anything I can do to help?" an unmistakable male voice taunted from the doorway.

Cassandra stared at Adam's mirrored reflection briefly before turning swiftly toward him, the instrument continuing its descent to the polished floor. She made no move to pick it up, fearful that in the attempt she might expose more than she hid. Cassandra said nothing, trying to avoid the subsequent expulsion of the remaining foam. Color rose in her cheeks as she swung back around and finished her toilet.

"You're early!" she accused, once it was safe for her to speak.

"A little," Adam admitted, his smile still broad as he walked into the room. "Triana knows the floor nurse and she gave us the okay."

125

Adam was formally attired. The dark charcoal tuxedo sat well upon his broad shoulders, the pale gray of the slightly ruffled shirt complementing the silver streaks in his hair. Evidently the party to which he was escorting Carlos Valdez's daughter was no small gathering as he'd led Cassandra to believe; rather, a major social event. Most likely it would be chronicled in the society section of the next day's newspaper, and the thought of waking to find a picture of Triana and Adam together caused Cassandra to wince.

A short distance down the hall, two women's voices could be heard in animated conversation, one of them unmistakably Triana's; the other, the nurse she had persuaded to bend the rules. Nurse Lopez probably thought she was doing Cassandra a favor when she allowed her visitors in early, not realizing that her actions would cause her patient intense embarrassment.

"That'll be Triana," Adam asserted unnecessarily.

"I know."

Stepping over the toothbrush, Cassandra's bare feet padded across the floor, her one hand still clutching at her gown and the other steering the metal pole whose wheels seemed bent on going in every direction but the one leading to her bed.

"Don't you dare!" Cassandra warned as she saw those blue eyes light up in anticipation of the difficulty she was going to have sliding back onto her perch gracefully. "Don't you laugh, Adam Ralston. . . . It was you who checked me into this–this–hotel!"

"Hospital," he corrected, countering her sarcasm. "In hotels you have to provide your own clothes . . . without southern exposures."

Glaring at Adam, Cassandra determined to ignore his chuckling. Checking to see that all flaps were secure, she then backed into the narrow space

126

between the beds. Her initial attempt was aborted, but on the second try she managed to land her bottom squarely on the firm mattress. Swinging her legs up, she covered them with the sheet and then inched the pole closer to allow her arm more freedom of movement. Leaning back against the elevated head section, a satisfied smile curved Cassandra's lips. She had at least been able to preserve a modicum of dignity.

At that precise moment a glittering cloud of black taffeta flowed into the room, the rich full skirt swinging about Triana's ankles. Hand-embroidered irridescent beading in a deep blue and true black covered the bodice of the gown, and the puffed taffeta sleeves gathered just below the elbow. The effect was stunning! While Cassandra knew that such a combination of fabrics and ornamentation would have been overpowering to her own fair coloring, on Triana the gown was marvelous. Artistically applied cosmetics enlivened the girl's olive complexion, while her raven locks glistened without adornment, their length cascading down over her shoulders.

Appraising Cassandra's jaundiced complexion and disheveled appearance, Triana could not restrain a smug smile of satisfaction. Even Cassandra had to admit that on this night Triana held the upper hand.

After placing the flowers she'd brought on the nearby table, Triana walked back to Adam and placed a possessive arm around his waist. "Adam tells me that you only got out of isolation today. I thought you might be needing something to brighten the room." Triana's words were sickeningly sweet. "It's good to see you looking so *well.*"

Cassandra chose to ignore the dig, hoping to keep peace between them. It was what Adam wanted. It was what God would want, too.

"Thank you," Cassandra returned genuinely, leaning over to inhale the fragrance of the colorful arrangement. "Just what I needed. They couldn't make these rooms drabber if they tried."

"This *is* a hospital," Adam reminded her.

"But I don't like hospitals," she countered, recalling his earlier retort as well.

"I know." His eyes played with the corners of her mouth. "You like hotels better."

The color rushed back into Cassandra's cheeks as she stole a glance at Triana and wondered what she must be thinking since she had not been present to hear the original innocent exchange. The girl's icy expression confirmed the impression that her thoughts were mutinous.

Sniffing at the antiseptic smell in the air, Triana herself changed the subject. "My mother . . . that is my *real* mother used to do some volunteer work in this hospital when I was a young girl." Her voice softened as her thoughts turned to happier times. "I knew Rosa, that is Nurse Lopez, when I was fourteen or so. I asked her to let us see you early as we have an important party to attend."

Cassandra wasn't sure whether Triana was offering an explanation for their sudden appearance, or searching for an excuse to leave.

"I'm glad you came," Cassandra stated politely. "But don't let me keep you from the party. I only wish I were well enough to be attending one myself." After a moment's thought, she added, "I've been meaning to compliment you on the lovely party in Butuan." Her words of praise brought an appreciative smile to Adam's face.

Fidgeting with the cloth-covered buckle at her waist, Triana said nothing. Her dark eyes darted to Adam, but remained only a second before shifting to Cassandra. The atmosphere was thoughtful rather than tense. "Thank you," she finally said grudgingly.

"I'm glad you enjoyed it." Her transparent expression revealed that she was openly speculative as to what had motivated Cassandra's kind remarks in return for her rude one. "I hope you'll be able to attend many more. But, of course, your work might make that difficult."

"Even a missionary needs to have some fun every once in a while," Adam interjected. "Don't you agree, Triana?"

Again Cassandra received a warning look from those black eyes. "That depends on the missionary . . . and the fun." Though Triana did not extend her gaze to include Adam, Cassandra was well aware that he was the subject of her words. "One's conduct, even in the area of recreation, must be such as not to offend the supporters back home . . . or the patrons on the field. Am I right?"

There was no doubt that Carlos Valdez's daughter could make trouble, and Cassandra knew it. She knew also what a reversal of Valdez's decision would mean to the mission enterprise, but she wasn't the kind to accept blackmail. "Missionaries do not work for their supporters, or their patrons . . . they work for their Lord."

"How noble!" Triana scoffed.

"That's enough!" Adam's words surprised them both.

The silence in the room was offset by the increasing noise level just beyond the door. Visiting hours were beginning, and an interesting blend of voices could be heard as visitors made their daily pilgrimage to the rooms of relatives and friends. The hard lump in Cassandra's throat prevented her from uttering a sound.

Adam was clearly angry, but she wasn't sure why. Was it because of Triana's hateful words, or her own response. She hadn't meant to sound so pious, but she was certain that was the way Adam would have interpreted it. Now she had botched what little chance there had ever been of being friends with Triana Valdez.

"I'm sorry," Cassandra finally managed, her eyes pleading for understanding.

"For what?" Adam's stern gaze was fixed on Triana. "You forget, dear, I've known you for too long not to be able to read your little games." Walking toward Cassandra, he placed a protective arm around her shoulders, then squarely addressed the beautiful young woman standing near the foot of the bed. "I love you, Triana, but if I ever hear of you launching another attack on Cassandra, you'll have to answer to *me*. I might even forget that you aren't a child anymore and take you over my knee."

The wide eyes of the sophisticated beauty betrayed her fear that he might do just that. "I didn't mean—"

"I know what you meant!" His statement was emphatic, and Triana made no more attempts to defend herself. "Now, say good night to Cassandra."

"Good night," she complied, her tone less than sincere.

How sad, thought Cassandra. *Two women in love with one man. Triana wants Adam's love, but can't have it. I want his love, but can't accept it. If nothing changes, all three of us will lose.*

"Good night," Adam whispered against her brow, softly kissing her forehead, before turning and gently guiding Triana out the door.

Without the pill that the nurses had insisted on giving her, there would have been no rest for Cassandra that night. Her mind was still groggy as she sought to identify the source of the insistent ringing in her head.

130

"The phone!" an impatient aide shouted through the opened door. "Get the phone."

"What?" Cassandra mumbled, struggling vainly to focus on the fuzzy white figure that was coming closer. "What did you say?"

With an exaggerated sigh, the woman lifted the heavy black receiver and thrust it into Cassandra's hand. "The phone!"

"Oh!" Sitting up with a start, she placed it to her ear, smiling her apology to the retreating figure. "Hello," she ventured meekly, wondering who would be calling her before she had even had her breakfast.

"Cassandra?" questioned the other party. "Cassandra Wellsley?"

"Speaking," she yawned.

"This is Sharon, from headquarters."

"Sharon Rhodes?"

"Yes. I called to warn you." The voice on the other end was almost conspiratorial.

"Something wrong?" Cassandra had gone through language school with Sharon and knew that she wasn't an alarmist. "Has something happened? Is Jodi okay?"

"Jodi is fine, but I did get a call this morning from *one irate Aunt Ernestine!*" Sharon's delivery would have been comical if her message had been more welcome. "The phone was ringing when I unlocked the office. I don't know how long she'd been trying to reach us."

"Is she in Manila now?" Aunt Ernestine on the heels of the emotional confrontation with Triana and Adam was almost more than she could handle. "How long has she been in the Philippines?"

"From the way she was carrying on, you would have thought she'd been here for months, but actually she arrived only night before last. She had evidently sent you a wire and expected you to be at the airport to greet her. She had to go to Pagsanjan yesterday for a layout at the falls. It seems she also expected you to join them there. Then when she heard you were ill . . . well, she's on her way back to Manila right now and will be pouncing on you when visiting hours begin." Sharon paused, giving Cassandra a moment to guess why Ernestine Powers was particularly disappointed that she hadn't gone on their photographic excursion. "She was really livid when I told her you were in the hospital. She screamed at me like it was all my fault that you were in the jungle. She sounds just like her letters."

"Poor Aunt Ernestine," Cassandra sighed. "She has always been strong-willed, but since Melinda's death, she's been impossible. Still, I can remember some fun times we had together."

"Well," Sharon hedged, her voice skeptical, "I wouldn't bet on this being one of them."

After hanging up, Cassandra almost wished that Sharon hadn't called to warn her. Now she had two hours to wait for the bomb to hit. The only edge it gave her was time to practice her responses to her aunt's predictable insistence that she give up the mission and return to modeling. Cassandra felt certain that she had planned for her to go to Pagsanjan Falls so that she could be included in some of the shots. Ernestine Powers talked about modeling as if it were a persistent amoeba—once you'd contracted the bug, it was difficult to get rid of it. What she kept forgetting, or refused to accept, was that Cassandra had never wanted to model in the first place.

Morals had never entered into her decision to leave the field, unless one counted the moral issue of doing what you feel is right with your life and not what someone else wants you to do. Cassandra had certainly never been asked to pose in a garment or a manner that would compromise her convictions or her dignity.

Her aunt had been adamant about that from the start. Randolph Martin required such conformity of some of his models, but never of Cassandra. Ernestine Powers was a force that not even he wanted to reckon with.

"Clean sensuality doesn't sell," Cassandra remembered her aunt quoting one of the clothiers whose account she had turned down. Now, three years after starting her own agency, Aunt Ernestine's success was assured, precisely because of her revolutionary philosophy. She had sold 'clean sensuality' in a way that no one else had been able to.

"My job is to dress, not to *undress* the female figure," her aunt had stated. "If an outfit has to be only half there to be alluring, then it is the work of a lazy designer. Where's the art in that? Pornography has been doing that for years!"

A tiny smile crept across Cassandra's face as she thought of seeing this woman again after so many years. The encounter with her aunt would be anything but dull! In fact, a morning spent with her would make Cassandra glad of the quieter hospital routine, not to mention helping to distract her from thoughts of Adam, however briefly.

Adam hadn't said he would be by to see her today, but Cassandra hoped so. She needed to discuss his mismanagement of the Triana situation. Cassandra had even felt sorry for the girl. She was flattered that Adam felt a need to defend her, but it hadn't been necessary to demoralize Triana in the process.

The phone rang again after she had finished her breakfast and the vampires from the lab had returned to their cave to run tests on the gallons of blood they had extracted. As she picked up the receiver, she wondered how she was left with enough strength to do so.

"Hel-lo," she exaggerated in a poor imitation of Bela Lugosi, her mood strangely light.

"And to whom am I speaking?" Adam laughed on the other end.

"Count Dracula," she scolded good-naturedly. "Don't you think they should have cast me instead of Bela Lugosi?"

"Frankly—no! You're much too pretty!"

"But the voice—what about the voice?"

"Are you up to having some company?" he side-stepped neatly. "You going to be around or do you have a heavy date?"

"Chicken!" Cassandra laughed. "See if I invite you to my Broadway opening!"

"Is that a promise?"

They laughed at the ridiculous sparring, both of them aware that they were simply postponing the conflicts that stood between them. It was at these times that Cassandra's heart swelled so that it was impossible for her to deny her love for Adam.

"No judge of talent, are you?"

"That depends." Adam's husky tone caused Cassandra to hug the receiver closer. "You have a great many talents . . . perhaps we can discuss some of them when I get to the hospital."

"My aunt might find that stimulating," she teased, wondering if his expression had changed upon hearing her announcement. "She called the mission and I understand that she will be here this morning, too. Did I ever tell you about my Aunt Ernestine?"

For a fleeting moment Cassandra thought about asking Adam not to come. The two of them would pose a formidable team—if Aunt Ernestine decided to enlist Adam in her cause to persuade Cassandra to leave the mission field. He just might agree—for different reasons. She was already aware that he believed she needed an extended leave to regain her health.

"Isn't she the model?" Adam inquired.

134

"Used to be," Cassandra corrected. "She has an agency now."

"Well, if she is anything like you, it will be a delight to meet her. Is she as beautiful as her niece?"

"Far more beautiful," she stated truthfully. "I'm afraid the main characteristic I inherited from Aunt Ernestine is her temper, but unlike me she makes no effort to control it. You might be safer if you waited until afternoon visiting hours. I understand from one of my friends at headquarters that she's on the warpath."

"Then maybe I ought to be there to make sure she doesn't take any scalps." His jovial manner recalled his defense of Cassandra only the night before. "Or are you afraid that I might be the one taking her scalp?"

"No . . ." Cassandra stated hesitantly, her mood becoming more somber as she weighed the possibilities. "If the two of you get together, the scalp taken just might be mine!"

CHAPTER 11

"FINALLY!" Ernestine Powers sighed, sailing into the hospital room and placing a perfunctory kiss on her niece's cheek. "Do you know what I had to go through to find you?"

Unsnapping the clasps of her royal purple earrings, she deposited them in her soft leather bag. Then, without waiting for an invitation, she availed herself of the remaining chair nearest Cassandra's bed. "You aren't surprised to see me, so I assume that mouse of a girl I talked to this morning called to say I was coming."

"Sharon called." Cassandra knew that there was nothing to be gained by speaking up for her co-worker. "She said you'd sent a wire wanting me to meet you."

"What else did she say?" Ernestine's brows lifted a fraction as she took in the handsome stranger occupying the chair on the opposite side of Cassandra's bed. "Never mind," she dismissed. "It was nothing important, I'm sure."

"Aunt Ernestine, I'd like you to meet Adam Ralston." Cassandra made the introduction almost reluctantly.

"I'm very pleased to meet you, Mrs. Powers." Adam's warm words were met with cold disdain. "Cassandra has spoken of you often."

"Humpf." Removing a hairpin from her tightly wound bun, Ernestine forced an errant tendril of glossy black hair back into place. "Is it really necessary that *he* be here during our conversation?"

Ignoring her rude dismissal, Adam rose voluntarily and headed for the door. "I'll be around if you need me," he directed at Cassandra, his smile reassuring.

"Nice-looking man." Ernestine's comment waited until Adam had left the room and closed the door behind him. "Did I tell you that we've started taking on a few accounts with men's lines? Claude has been searching for someone like your friend. . . . Adam was it? Has he ever done any modeling?"

"No . . . I wouldn't think so."

"Too bad. He'd photograph well. . . . That heavy beard would require some touching up, but otherwise he's perfect." Cassandra remained silent, choosing not to interrupt her aunt's monologue. "You remember Claude . . . I stole him away from Randolph. He's with me on this trip." Shifting in her seat, Ernestine slipped out of her jacket, revealing more of the delicately swirled pattern of the lavender and plum in her short-sleeved boatneck blouse. "Give me your friend's phone number, and I might give him a call."

"Adam wouldn't be interested," Cassandra insisted.

"Are you his keeper? . . . Oh, never mind." With an impatient gesture, she dismissed the idea. "If he's one of your pious little friends, you're probably right. The whole lot of you would rather live off other people's charity than work for a living."

138

"Aunt Ernestine!" Cassandra couldn't believe her ears. "Just what do you think we do with our days—drink tea and eat crumpets?"

"Hardly!" she snorted, the green of her eyes flashing amber sparks. "Look at you! You could be one of the most famous models ever; I could still make it happen for you. Instead, you toil away in some jungle for three years teaching filthy illiterates some idealistic ideology that can't help them, and has surely not helped you!"

Rising, she leaned over her niece's bed, continuing her tirade. "You labor, you toil, you ruin your health—but for what? What do you accomplish? Work must have something tangible to show for it."

Extracting a gold monogrammed case from her purse, Ernestine quickly snapped open the lid and brought a cigarette to her lips. "Personally," she began, using her matching lighter and then pausing to take a long draw. "Personally, I don't care if some misguided group of do-gooders wants to spend their hard-earned money on this ridiculous farce, but I won't stand by and see you waste your life any longer." After inhaling once more, Ernestine's eyes darted about the room until she spotted a suitable container in which to extinguish her barely touched cigarette. "What would you really have to show after ten, twenty years in a tribe? All you'd have accomplished is to educate another group to the fairy tales of the Bible."

"They aren't fairy tales!" Blinking back the tears, Cassandra fought to stand her ground. "What we accomplish is far more tangible and lasting than the merchandising of this year's fashions. God is real, unchangeable, eternal—and anyone who needs Him can find Him."

"And where was your God when Melinda died?"

Guilt welled up in Cassandra as a tense silence

descended over the room. Her aunt didn't want to hear about how Cassandra had failed to prepare her daughter for eternity—she wanted to know why God had allowed her to die. Cassandra had also hoped right up to the end that Melinda would be spared. There was a chance that she had trusted Christ at the same youth camp where Cassandra's faith had had its beginning, but she'd never spoken of it. Somehow talking to her cousin about eternity when she was so sick had seemed to Cassandra like a sealing of the coffin—too final. Shouldn't she be cheerful and speak of trivialities—anything to keep the mood light and to give Melinda hope that she would recover? She had justified her silence then, but it had awakened her to the resolve never to justify her silence again.

"If Melinda were still alive, she would never have disappointed me like you have!"

"No," Cassandra stated softly, a single tear trailing down her cheek and pooling at the corner of her mouth. "Melinda wanted to be a model—just like her mother." Extracting a tissue from the bedstand box, Cassandra dabbed at her eyes. "I can't bring Melinda back, but Aunt Ernestine, I won't again accept the role of replacing her, either. I'm me—Cassandra Wellsley—not Melinda Powers."

"You could never replace Melinda! How dare you even imply that I ever entertained the possibility." Haughtily she snatched up her jacket and glared at her niece. "You could never fill Melinda's shoes!"

"But haven't you tried to force me into them?" The truth had to come out in the open if her aunt was ever to bury her daughter and let her niece live her own life. "While Melinda was alive, you never pressured me to model. I did it because Melinda was doing it, but your plans and dreams were for Melinda—not for me. Can't you see what you're doing?"

Confusion flashed across Ernestine's face, her

nostrils flaring for a second before releasing her breath. "I've done nothing. Nothing that a caring aunt wouldn't do." Picking up her purse, she stared at Cassandra in thoughtful silence. "I've not given up," she announced finally, her expression one of determination. "When I leave Manila, you are going with me."

"No, Aunt Ernestine," Cassandra whispered weakly, "when I leave the Philippines, it will be because I feel it is the right thing to do, not because you, or anyone else forces me to."

"You heard her!" Adam's masculine voice echoed from the doorway.

"And who do you think you are?" she spewed, venting her wrath on the man who had slipped unnoticed into the room.

With jaws set, the icy blue of Adam's eyes bore into the cold emerald of hers. "Obviously someone who cares more about your niece's well-being than you do, Mrs. Powers."

"How dare you!"

"I'll dare a lot more if I ever find you upsetting Cassandra again."

"Upsetting her!" Ernestine blared. "I'm trying to bring her to her senses, make her see how she's wasting her life."

"How do *you* know it's a waste?" Adam walked closer to the bed, speaking calmly, his soft-spoken words defusing the volatile situation. "Do you really understand what Cassandra does?"

"I know enough!"

"I used to think I knew enough, too."

"What are you?" she shouted. "Another one of those Bible-thumpers who let God run their lives, instead of taking responsibility for it themselves?" Again a strand of dark hair escaped its forced confinement, but this time Ernestine Powers didn't bother to refasten it, hastily pushing it behind an ear, uncaring that it detracted from the total image she had tried so painstakingly to create.

Cassandra pulled the covers up around herself, tightly closing her eyes against the ugly scene. She could think of nothing to say to ease the tense moment. And though she was the main topic of discussion, she felt herself an outsider in the exchange. Her throat ached with suppressed emotion, her mind willing away the hysterical bubbles of sobs that threatened to emerge. To say anything would only insure their release.

When Cassandra opened her eyes, she was surprised to find a broad smile etching Adam's features. "Yes, Mrs. Powers, I guess that's just what I am," he admitted, referring to her accusation. "Only in reverse. I've been leaving God out and running my own life. It's been a long time since we have spoken the same language. Lately, I've been considering taking a refresher course." Shifting his gaze to Cassandra, Adam's eyes rested on her warmly. "Your niece once accused me of being a deserter of sorts. She said I was staging a retreat instead of fighting in the battle. Is that what you're doing, Mrs. Powers? Are you retreating from the battle?"

"What do *you* know?" Ernestine shouted, a flood of tears flowing down her cheeks. It was the first time Cassandra had seen her aunt cry. She hadn't even shed a tear at Melinda's funeral. "You don't know what it's like to lose a daughter."

Cassandra gasped, fearing the impact of her aunt's words on Adam, but she marveled at his control as he closed the distance between himself and Ernestine, taking her in a firm embrace. "You'd be surprised at all I've lost, Mrs. Powers—and I think a little surprised at some of the things you've never found."

Like a child, the proud Ernestine Powers allowed

Adam to lead her out of the door and down the hall. Cassandra watched in awe, replaying in her mind the words she had just heard Adam speak. She didn't want to read too much into their meaning, but they filled her with a hope that she knew was best not fanned. What she'd witnessed could mean everything—or nothing.

The storm had started around midnight, waking Cassandra out of a troubled sleep. For over an hour she'd stood by the window, mesmerized as it unleashed its fury. With the morning, it had gradually abated.

Grateful that she no longer had to deal with the awkward I.V., Cassandra slipped once more from her bed and returned to the window, watching as the bright sun turned the remaining droplets to glistening jewels of light. It was the calm after the storm that had renewed her spirits many times before. But this time she felt a leaden emptiness.

How silly to mope over the fact that Adam hadn't phoned or made an appearance since the morning before. Twice, following the evening visiting hours, Cassandra had dialed the number of the Valdez home, and twice she had plunked down the receiver after only one ring. If Adam Ralston wanted to talk to her, he'd call.

She could only guess at what her aunt and he had talked about, and for how long, but she doubted it had taken all of the day and evening, too. It was more than curiosity that prompted her need to speak with him. If he didn't contact her today, she would know that her feelings of disquiet were well-founded.

Scanning the still wet world below her, Cassandra noted the increased activity. The thrice-daily pilgrimage was beginning and she could only hope that Adam was one of those dodging the potholes and vying for a place to park his company vehicle. Nervously Cassandra twisted the tissue stretched between her two hands until the soft white paper became so tightly wound that she was forced to reverse the rotation.

"Please let him come," she quietly prayed, backing away from the window and reluctantly climbing into bed.

Several people passed Cassandra's door, but none resembled the one she most wanted to see. The staccato beat of slender heels against the polished linoleum announced the one visitor she preferred to avoid. She knew who it was even before her aunt rounded the corner. Defensively Cassandra pulled the covers up to her chin and turned her back.

"Cassandra?"

"Please, Aunt Ernestine," Cassandra pleaded without even turning around. "I don't want to argue any more . . . I'm not leaving the mission."

"I didn't come to argue," she stated in a gentler tone than Cassandra had heard in years. "I came to apologize."

Total silence reigned as Cassandra registered her aunt's words and slowly shifted her body. "What?" she asked in disbelief, daring to look into the older woman's eyes. "What did you say?"

"I came to apologize," Ernestine repeated with a smile. "You were right. I have been using you as a substitute for Melinda—but no more . . . never again." Moving closer, she set aside her purse and the shiny foil package she was carrying and eagerly enfolded her niece in her arms. "Can you forgive me?"

The warm embrace brought tears to both the women's eyes as they clung to one another. "Of course," Cassandra sniffed, hugging her aunt to her. With the tortured remnant of her tissue, Cassandra dabbed futilely at her own tears, then at the dark

144

blotches forming on her aunt's rich silk blouse. "I'm sorry . . . I'm ruining your beautiful blouse."

"I'm not," Ernestine smiled. "If it stains, I'll just keep it as a souvenir."

"Of what? . . . A blubbering niece?"

"Yes . . . and a very happy aunt!" Taking a beautifully embroidered handkerchief and tortoise shell compact from her snakeskin bag, Ernestine Powers began to repair her own damage. "It wouldn't do for that young man of yours to see his latest convert looking like 'Apple Annie'."

"Exactly what did you and Adam talk about yesterday?"

"You mean after I stopped screaming at him?" she questioned with a wry grin. "I think if I'd been a man he would have belted me, instead of giving me his shoulder to cry on. I sure have been doing a lot of crying these last two days." Snapping the compact closed, she returned it to her purse. "Your uncle is not going to believe any of this when I tell him. During our last argument he said that I couldn't get any harder if I turned to stone . . . and he was right." Lifting the package from the chair, she sat down and rested it on her lap. "Why he's stayed with me all these years, I'll never know."

"He loves you," Cassandra stated simply.

"Just like your Adam."

"He's not mine," Cassandra hedged. "And as for love—"

"He's got it bad."

"Did he tell you he loved me?"

"Not in so many words, but I've been around for over . . . well, a long time," Ernestine chuckled. "I don't need a man to put into words what I read in his eyes and see in his actions. I think you're smart enough to know the answer to your own question.

And I hope that you're smart enough to hang on to him. Adam Ralston is a rare find these days."

"You don't understand," Cassandra groaned, burying her face in her hands.

"I understand a lot more about a lot of things. . . . Two days ago you would have been right, but not now." A knowing smile greeted Cassandra as she lifted her eyes to meet her aunt's twinkling ones. "I understand why you became a missionary—and I approve."

"You *do* ?"

"Yes." Ernestine's grin broadened at her niece's astonished look. "I can't honestly give Adam Ralston all the credit. You and the Sanderses gave my armor enough dents over the years, but it took someone who had suffered in the same way that I had to make me face the truth."

"Adam told you about his wife and daughter?"

"And about his medical training, and about giving it all up after they died. . . . Did you know he was going to be a medical missionary?" Cassandra's eyes were wide. "I didn't think so," her aunt continued. "I don't think he meant to tell me, either. It just slipped out. In a way, I think nearly everything he said that really mattered just slipped out."

"What else did he say?" Cassandra was surprised that her numbed brain could function well enough to form the words.

Glancing at her watch, Ernestine looked uncertain. "I really ought to let him tell you. I've probably said too much already." Biting down on her lip, she thought for a moment before speaking. "It was strange. I felt that as Adam was sharing with me the message of God's love, he was beginning to believe it again himself . . . I don't mean the fundamentals, but the broader principle. He acted like that young man in the *Bible* who blew his life's savings, and then went back to his dad who, instead of kicking him out of the family, threw him a big party.''

"The prodigal son,'' Cassandra supplied.

"Yes, that's the one,'' Ernestine nodded. "Only Adam seemed afraid, or reluctant, or something. He was like that son, but he hadn't decided to go home yet. . . . Does what I'm saying make any sense?''

"In a way,'' Cassandra assured her. "Adam's pretty close-mouthed about his past. What you've said fills in some of the blanks. I've suspected for a long time that he was a Christian, and now I know it's true. I guess that's something . . . but it's just not enough, Aunt Ernestine.''

"Be patient, my dear. Adam's seen something in you that's made him want again what he used to have. People who haven't stumbled in life don't realize how hard it is to get up and start over.'' Nervously Ernestine rotated the diamond-encrusted wedding band around her finger. "It's not that we like where we are, but change is such a big step. I don't even know how I'm going to fare. I think it was the imperfect state of Adam's faith that gave me the courage to ask the questions I'd been on the verge of asking you for years.''

"You never seemed interested before,'' Cassandra stated meekly, intrigued by this more serious side of her aunt. "In fact, you got angry every time I mentioned God.''

"No,'' Ernestine disagreed. "I got *furious*! When Melinda died I was mad at the whole world, but it was God I hated most. Then you came along, and instead of hating God, too, you announced that you wanted to spend your whole life serving Him in some forsaken place I'd never heard of. I was torn between hating you for being a traitor, and loving you enough to want to save you from yourself.''

Accepting her unspoken invitation, Ernestine firmly

grasped her niece's hand. "It was Melinda's death that decided me on missions," Cassandra said softly.

"I'm glad," Ernestine Powers smiled. "I'm glad her death served some purpose. I'm no longer bitter, Cassandra. Now I can go home and grieve properly, as I should have done all those years ago."

"Stay awhile," Cassandra pleaded, her eyes warm with the need to share so much. "I should be out of here in a few days. You could go back to the tribe with me and I could show you what we do there. In a way, it's Melinda's work, too. I want you to meet my partner Jodi, and the natives. You'd like Fely—she can be as stubborn as you at times! And there's Marta, and the new baby. She named her Cassandra. . . ."

"I'd love to, dear." Ernestine's eyes were no longer hard as on that first day, but shimmered with a new warmth. "But I can't. I have so much catching up to do that I don't know where to start. I have a husband whom I hardly know anymore, a son, and two grandbabies who don't know their grandmother. . . . I never realized until yesterday how much pain I must have brought to them all. I've been selfish, willful—you name it. I can't promise a miracle change, even now, but at least I've a place to start, and a God who will teach me as I go along."

"I'll miss you," Cassandra whispered, giving her aunt's hand one final squeeze before releasing it. "When do you plan to leave?"

"Today!"

"Today?"

"Yes, I can't wait to begin my new life! I have such good news to tell my family that I want to shout! I never knew anything could feel so wonderful!" Ernestine's face was bright with irrepressible joy. "If you hear that your uncle has sent me to a looney farm, you'll have to come to my defense. I just hope his heart is strong enough to take the new me."

"Maybe you should tell him in stages," Cassandra laughed, her aunt's excitement contagious.

"Do I look like the kind of woman who does anything in stages?" With a deep sigh she glanced impatiently at her watch. "I still have to pack, and inform poor Claude that he's on his own."

"Are you quitting the agency?" Disbelief showed on Cassandra's face.

"No," her aunt assured her. "But if I'm going to become a real wife, and get to know my son's children before they're grown, I can't be flitting around the world. I'll go in half-days to make sure my standards are being observed, but the agency is not going to *be* my life anymore!"

"How's Claude going to take the news?"

"Claude?" Ernestine's brows knit together as she pondered the question. "I doubt he'll really mind, but he will probably make a show of being peeved and claim that he can't function without me. With Claude, I might have to break the news gently, especially in the area of my *reason*. I'm ashamed to say that the two of us have had more than one 'God' roast over the years."

"I remember what he told me when I left modeling."

"I can imagine," Ernestine inserted. "We have also had a few 'Cassandra's a fool' sessions. I think the fellow might just faint when he learns I've joined the enemy camp."

"George will be happy . . . it's too bad you don't have time to fly over and see him."

"Give him my love," Ernestine teased. "But make sure he's sitting down when you tell him, or you're liable to have to scrape him off the floor, too. George is one man I've maligned more than a person should ever be forgiven for.''

Cassandra was well aware that there had always been a soft place in George Sanders' heart for Ernestine Powers, and that he had never ceased praying for her. He would be overjoyed to hear that she had finally trusted Christ.

Cassandra didn't want to say goodbye, but she understood her Aunt Ernestine's need to repair broken bridges and to start her new life. ''When will I see you again?''

''From what I heard the doctor say to Adam yesterday, you should be going with me.'' The admonishment was less severe than it would have been even twenty-four hours before, but the expression of concern was greater. ''You really should think about it, Cassandra. You need to rest, to regain your strength. If you'll do it, I'll put off my flight until you're discharged, and I'll even buy you a round-trip ticket. You can consider it a vacation. . . . Please?''

There was wisdom in her aunt's words, not that Cassandra hadn't heard the same advice before. But she wasn't ready to leave. And though she felt an obligation to her work with the tribe, Cassandra knew there was more—much more. There had been more ever since that day nearly six weeks ago—the day she had met Adam Ralston. If she left now, it would almost certainly end their fragile relationship—before it had a chance to develop. And if there were even a remote chance . . . No, she couldn't leave—not yet.

''I can't,'' Cassandra whispered, noting the disappointment in her aunt's eyes. ''I just can't.''

CHAPTER 12

TEAL HAD ALWAYS BEEN A GOOD COLOR on her, Cassandra acknowledged, running her hand down the satiny finish of the gown and matching robe. Peering into the small mirrored cabinet, she viewed a much-improved patient and was grateful to her aunt for the thoughtful gifts. The blush on her cheeks and the tinge of color above her eyes further masked her still slightly jaundiced complexion. She regretted that her aunt hadn't the time to stick around and see her in the lovely ensemble.

Ernestine Powers' plane had taken off an hour ago, after she had called from the terminal to say her final goodbyes and make one last plea for her niece to change her mind about accompanying her. Cassandra wondered when they would ever see each other again. Her aunt had promised to visit soon, but had made no specific commitment. Cassandra doubted that she would return that year, and by the next year she felt certain that the mission would insist that she take her furlough.

151

Her aunt had been right about a lot of things, she realized. Adam's thinking *had* mellowed quite a bit in the time she had known him. He had set aside his bitterness toward God long enough to share Him with another—surely that was a positive sign. She didn't honestly know what it was like to turn away from God, and then battle with the decision to start on the road back to fellowship with Him. How could she presume to judge or put a timetable on what she had never experienced?

The greatest temptations of Cassandra's own Christian life had come in the last month or so in the form of Adam Ralston. The thought of living a life without him brought a physical pain greater than any she had suffered through her illness. Yet each day was a battle to adhere to the standards of her faith. It would be so easy to tell him of her love and accept his limited views as enough to see them through.

So easy, her mind repeated as she walked to the window and searched for the first evening star. *Star light, star bright. . . .* But superstitious little rhymes held no real power, she knew. The power for change was not in the creation, but in the Creator. As one pinprick of light after another appeared in the dark canopy above, she wondered how many foolish wishes were being made upon the beacons of fiery gas. How sad that so many still trusted in impotent gods—even those as innocent as stars in the night sky.

Shifting her gaze, Cassandra focused her thoughts on the vehicles leaving the visitors' parking lot. Twenty minutes still remained of visiting hours, and a small stream of cars rushed in to beat the cut-off while the larger group was exiting. To her disappointment, Adam hadn't come. It was too dark now to make out the individual cars, but she doubted that he was among the late arrivals.

Cassandra knew that Adam and her doctor had discussed her condition and had decided what she should do when she was released from the hospital in two days time. But she wasn't going to do it! Adam would be furious with her when she refused to return home to the States. But home for her now was that crude structure that she shared with Jodi back in the jungle, not the fancy house where her parents lived in Louisiana. This was her Eden, and though she knew that modern technology might destroy it some day, this was her life and her work and she intended to stay until she was driven out!

Since meeting Adam, however, there had been a certain restlessness that not even her work with the tribe could completely satisfy. Going back wouldn't solve all her problems, she admitted, but there was no place on the face of the earth where she could run that would erase Adam Ralston from her mind and heart. She must simply work harder and longer and devote herself completely to the people she had come to know and love as her own.

A tear born of frustration trickled down the side of Cassandra's face. Wiping it away, she walked slowly back to the bed. Visiting hours were all but over now. A quick glance at her watch confirmed the time, and she idly watched the departing visitors passing her door. Leaning back against the pillow, Cassandra closed her eyes tightly, listening to the footsteps in the hall and trying to stay the remaining tears that begged for release. Crying only left her eyes swollen and red, she tried to convince herself as a disobedient drop of moisture escaped its bounds. Tears wouldn't bring Adam back to God, she reasoned, nor would they bring him into her presence.

Cassandra blotted away the droplet as it turned the corner of her cheek and headed down to trace her jawline.

"Don't cry . . ." coaxed a gentle voice, causing her to sniff back a sob and open her eyes wide. "I can't stand to see you cry."

"Adam—" The lines etched around his mouth seemed deeper, and his features drained. "Adam," she repeated, allowing herself to be gathered up in his arms. "I . . . I—"

"Don't speak," he commanded, holding her from him and gazing into her face. "I have so much I want to say, and so much that I must school myself not to say." His brows shot up as he took in her improved appearance. "With you looking so lovely I can tell that this isn't going to be easy." Lazily Adam brought a hand up to wipe away the remnants of moisture that had settled upon the ledge of Cassandra's lower lashes. "I talked the nurse into giving me an extra fifteen minutes, but I wish that I'd asked for *much* longer."

With his right hand already cupping her chin, Adam used the left to gently shift Cassandra's head, positioning her eager lips to receive his feather-light kiss. Then, with a deep sigh of resolution, he gently pushed her back against the pillow. "How can I say good-bye?" The words were torn from him, no answer offered or expected.

Impetuously Cassandra reached for him, twining her arms behind his neck, playing with the curls at its nape. A small cry of pleasure escaped her parted lips as Adam bent to drop another kiss on the creamy skin of her slender neck.

Then taking Cassandra's arms from around his neck, Adam squeezed her hands in his, bringing them to his lips. For endless moments he held her eyes steadily with his own. "When you get to Louisiana you'll soon forget about the arrogant logger who gave you such a hard time. . . ." His voice choked to a whisper. "But I'll never forget one fiery missionary. . . ." With determined effort he tried to initiate a lighter mood. "I still have a score to settle with George Sanders for not warning me when he sent me to see you that first time. They ought to make you wear a label: Open at your own risk. Highly explosive. Life-changing. May be fatal if taken into your heart." Then the expression on Adam's face sobered again as he rose to his feet. "Maybe you won't even come back. There are probably a half-dozen guys sitting around back home, wondering how they ever let you get away the first time. I already know that I'll be calling myself a fool in the morning for letting you get away now."

All the love that Cassandra felt for Adam welled up inside her as she studied his beloved face, now haggard and worn. "You didn't get much sleep last night, did you?"

"No, I've had a lot on my mind. . . ." With that now familiar gesture, he raked his hand through his hair. "I'll sleep easier when I know that you're on a plane away from here."

"I'm not going," Cassandra stated firmly.

"Don't push me," Adam warned. "I know you think that everything changed with my little discussion with your aunt . . . but it didn't." His eyes told her that what he said was true. "I only wish it had."

"But surely it meant something," she argued.

"Not enough," Adam countered. "I've been there, it's true—I'm sure your aunt told you that part." Adam turned and walked to the window where Cassandra had spent so much of her time wondering about the future. "I know what you need, but I can't give it to you—"

"But you can!"

"Maybe once," he conceded, his eyes gazing out into the darkness. "And maybe again—someday."

For moments Adam stood, saying nothing. With

hands thrust into his pockets, he turned and started back toward the bed. "I felt good about what happened with your aunt . . . but it wasn't planned . . . and might not ever happen again."

Taking Cassandra's hand in his, he gently traced the feathery veins with his fingers, drinking in her lovely features as if memorizing them. A thin line of control stretched between them as he leaned forward and gave Cassandra a final kiss. "Go home Cassandra," he pleaded, "Go home while I still have the strength to ask you to leave."

Silently Cassandra skimmed the lines of fine blue handwriting filling the pages of ivory vellum.

"What does Ernestine have to say?" Jodi asked, eagerly peering over Cassandra's shoulder. "Did your uncle faint at the news?"

"No, but it seems that her daughter-in-law almost did. Aunt Ernestine showed up one morning and volunteered to sit with the boys for a few hours," Cassandra laughed, flipping to the second page of her aunt's letter. "She actually enjoyed her time with them and says she plans to see them often. It's hard to believe that this is the same woman who stormed into my hospital room two weeks ago. . . . I wish Adam could read this!"

Moving around to the opposite side of the couch, Jodi plopped down next to her roommate, unaware of the direction in which Cassandra's thoughts had turned. Extending her right hand, Jodi wiggled her fingers impatiently at her friend. "Well, are you going to let me read it or not?" she complained.

"What?" Cassandra questioned, her mind far away.

"The letter!" Jodi's brows drew together in a puzzled frown. "Are you reading—or maybe thinking about Adam Ralston? I've wondered about that look

156

that comes into your eyes every time his name is mentioned.''

Riffling through the sheets in her hand, Cassandra withdrew the two she'd finished and thrust them into Jodi's hand. "Here—this should get you started." Dropping her eyes, she pretended to concentrate on the missive before her. Although she had told Jodi about Adam's part in Ernestine Powers' coming to Christ, the confidences had gone no further.

"My cousin Arlene used to get that look every time I mentioned the name John Tyler. Unfortunately John Tyler never got that look when I mentioned Arlene!" A devilish grin inched its way across Jodi's face as she speculated upon the true nature of the relationship between Cassandra and Adam. "What kind of look does Adam get when *your* name is mentioned?"

Stubbornly Cassandra refused to glance up, or to acknowledge Jodi's question. She didn't want to talk about Adam Ralston. With a sigh of resignation, Jodi gave up for the moment.

Silencing Jodi was one thing, but silencing her own thoughts was quite another, Cassandra realized with dismay. Adam hadn't contacted Cassandra since that night at the hospital when she had refused his advice and told him that she was returning to the tribe. She had expected him to be angry, but his reaction had been one of disappointment instead. He had casually informed her that he was leaving the next morning for Butuan, and had offered to contact the mission about arrangements for her transport since he would not be able to escort her himself.

He hadn't even called the next day to say goodbye. If not for the news that she received from George, she wouldn't know anything at all about Adam Ralston's whereabouts. After Butuan Cassandra learned that he'd gone back to the field base briefly and then out to the new site. She wasn't sure if he had asked George to keep her posted, or if George had just sensed her need to know.

What she'd learned during the last week, however, had Cassandra worried. Two local rebel leaders had been arrested and George had reluctantly admitted that there was a substantial increase in the number of violent threats being received at headquarters. Adam reportedly was working near one of the areas where widespread fighting was raging. Cassandra tried not to fear for Adam's safety and yield her concern to the Lord.

After reading the same paragraph for the third time, Cassandra decided to give up on the letter. "Here," she stated, depositing the last two pages in Jodi's lap. "I'll finish it later. I have to go to the clinic anyway. Marta is bringing the baby in for a check-up."

"You ought to be resting," Jodi scolded, catching one of the sheets before it slid to the ground. "You promised the doctor you'd take a nap *every* afternoon."

Rising, Cassandra unfastened the clip at the back of her head, combing a few errant strands of golden brown hair into place with her long slender fingers. "I will—later," she assured a doubtful Jodi. Refastening the simple metal restraint, Cassandra slid her feet into her worn rubber thongs and slipped out the door.

"I'll tell!" Jodi yelled after the retreating figure.

Pausing halfway down the porch steps, a grudging smile of affection replaced Cassandra's worried frown. "Yes, Mother," she shot back over her shoulder. Since her illness Jodi had become a regular mother hen; Cassandra, the chick. "If I hurry I might even be back in bed before you have time to tell Daddy I've been naughty!"

Cassandra didn't have to see to know the face Jodi would be making. The thought of what her teammate would say to George Sanders when he made his usual afternoon call had Cassandra chuckling to herself all the way to the clinic.

A cool breeze swept across the open porch as Cassandra sat thinking about the group of women that would be arriving for their reading lesson within the hour. Picking up one of the graded readers, Cassandra curled her legs under her, Indian style, and began the job of scanning the material she wanted to cover that night. The woven bamboo seat creaked softly as she shifted, trying to find a more comfortable position.

Cassandra had nearly finished when she glanced up to find Jodi standing beside her, holding a fresh cup of tea in each hand. Smiling her thanks, Cassandra cleared a space on the tiny wooden table that stood between the two chairs. "Just put it here." The pathetic piece of furniture had seen better days, but neither Cassandra nor Jodi was willing to part with it. Weather and insects had taken their toll, but it had been their first gift from one of the native children and was, therefore, priceless.

"Is Marta coming?" Jodi placed the equally faded china on the slightly uneven surface, then settled into the other chair. "You never told me yesterday how the baby is doing."

"And *you* never told *me* the secret you and George are keeping from me." At first, Cassandra had thought it was her imagination, but in the last twenty-four hours both her friends had cleverly side-stepped every question she'd asked about Adam. "You haven't been yourself since I returned from the clinic yesterday—after George's call. As a matter of fact, this is the first time you've even asked about little Cassandra."

"I've been busy," Jodi hedged, picking up her teacup and sipping furiously at the steaming brew. "So, how is the baby?"

159

It was another ploy to change the subject, but Jodi wasn't going to get away with it this time! "The baby is fine and Marta will be here tonight. Now that we have that out of the way—"

"Is she sleeping through the night yet? One of my nieces didn't sleep through until she was almost five months old. My sister couldn't stand it, so she put her on cereal before bedtime, despite what her doctor said. When he objected, she told him he could come and give the baby the two o'clock feeding if he felt that strongly about it." Biting down nervously on her bottom lip, Jodi smiled tentatively, then took another sip. "Of course, when she put it that way he backed off. Personally, I think they did the right thing. You know how it is with doctors—every ten years or so, they throw out everything the last generation has believed about child care and go to the opposite extreme. One time it's breast milk . . . then it's the bottle . . . then it's solids right away . . ." Jodi paused for breath. "Well, I have a few things to do before the evening call, and I shouldn't be yakking anyway. You're busy. . . ."

"Sit down." Cassandra's words were spoken softly, compelling Jodi to obey. She had waited long enough to hear what she already sensed—had sensed for days.

"Couldn't we talk later?" Jodi shifted uncomfortably.

"Now," Cassandra demanded, folding the book that she'd been clutching during Jodi's little speech. Setting it on the rough planks next to her chair, Cassandra rose. Walking to the rail, she took several deep breaths and let them out again before turning to face her friend. "Where are they holding Adam?"

"They aren't!" Jodi blurted, setting down her cup abruptly. "At least we don't *know* that they are . . . I mean, there hasn't been any ransom note. . . . There

160

hasn't been anything . . . no one has heard from Adam in three days!"

"Three days," Cassandra repeated. "Surely the company. . ."

A shake of Jodi's head confirmed that they hadn't heard anything either.

"Are they searching for him? . . . What are they doing to find him?" Tears welled up in Cassandra's eyes as she thought of the man she loved possibly suffering the same fate of the other manager about this time a year ago. "If they get a ransom demand, will Pacific Lumber pay it?"

Jodi's eyes locked with those of her friend, a message of shared concern and Christian love filtering through. "I don't know," she managed, her own eyes filling with tears. "A Jonathan Sloan from the plant—"

"I know him."

"And the daughter of the president of the company—"

"Triana Valdez."

"Yes . . . I . . . well, I think that's the name George used." In her flustered state, Jodi's tongue tripped over the words. "Well, they came to see George yesterday morning and told him to report anything that might be a lead to Adam's whereabouts. They seemed genuinely concerned from what George said."

"But is the company concerned enough to pay a ransom?" Tentatively Jodi touched Cassandra's shoulder and Cassandra allowed herself to be folded into her friend's loving arms. "Will they pay it?" Cassandra cried, hugging Jodi even closer to her. "Or will they let him die?"

The beginning calls of the night creatures were a bizarre accompaniment to Cassandra's sobs. "I know it isn't company policy to give in to rebel demands, but, Jodi, they have to pay . . . they just have to!"

"But, Cass, we aren't even certain the rebels have him. Where's your faith?"

"Oh, Jodi, you're right!" Cassandra moaned, releasing her friend and turning to grip the ragged rail. Staring up into the starless night, Cassandra watched as a flash of lightning illuminated the sky and the roar of thunder pierced the stillness, as if in answer to her silent prayer. "I love him, Jodi . . . I love him so much!"

"Well, that wasn't so hard to figure out. Now, come inside," Jodi prompted. "You get ready for bed, and I'll take care of the ladies. Who knows, maybe in the morning he'll be back, and safe, and we'll all have worried for nothing."

"I hope so," Cassandra whispered. "Oh, I truly hope so."

CHAPTER 13

O YE OF LITTLE FAITH, the swollen-eyed reflection seemed to chide Cassandra as she stared into the mirror.

Was it just last night, or a hundred years ago that she'd learned of Adam's disappearance? Had it all been a nightmare from which she would soon awaken—or was it true? Were those haggard features in the mirror really hers? Splashing tepid water on her puffed lids, Cassandra looked once more. No one would judge her beautiful this morning!

The aroma of freshly brewed coffee greeted her as she finished up in the bathroom and headed into the kitchen.

"How are you feeling?" Handing Cassandra a steaming cup of fresh coffee, Jodi's eyes searched her friend's face, not really expecting an answer. "I heard you in the bathroom and thought I'd have it ready for you. It's our last, but George said last night that our supplies have been sent and are at the logging base."

"Did he say anything about Adam?"

Refilling her cup, Jodi motioned for Cassandra to come and sit with her at the table. "There is still no ransom demand . . . and by now there should have been. That Jonathan fellow was by again, and he seems to think the logging crew might have hid out someplace. Evidently headquarters hasn't heard from any of them."

Neither voiced the other possibility for the long, unbroken silence. "Are they sending someone out to search for them?"

"It's a big jungle, Cassandra. I'm sure they're doing as much as they can, but they can't go into the areas where there is fighting. . . ." Reaching across the table, Jodi squeezed her friend's hand. "A group is flying out to the field house today, so I don't know how first-hand George's information will be after that. Why don't you go with the men when we send them for supplies? You could talk with this Jonathan Sloan, and the president of the company—Valdez. I can take care of things here. If the man I loved were in danger, I know I'd want to be there."

Cassandra did want to be there. She was tempted to take Jodi up on her offer, but Cassandra knew that it wasn't her place. She fervently prayed that Adam was safe, and that his ordeal had somehow helped to draw him closer to God. If it had, then he would be coming to her and everything would truly work out right. What she needed now was patience and faith—patience to wait and faith to believe.

The house was cleaner than it had ever been. Even the latest shipment of supplies had been stowed in their proper places. There was nothing more Cassandra could do. Physical activity had helped to distract her temporarily, but the minutes had dragged by ever since the midday call from George. Jodi had been right. George had heard nothing more from the logging company since Jonathan Sloan's visit.

Pacing the office, Cassandra scolded herself for her lack of concentration. Abandoning the idea of drafting the monthly newsletter, she bent to retrieve the crumpled sheets of paper that lay on the floor. Tossing them into the wastebasket near the door, she looked up. Through the open door, she could see the path to the clinic; to her left, the lush green of the jungle beyond. Though no path was cut in that direction, Cassandra recalled a lovely little clearing that wandered off the main trail, where Adam had taken her on his second visit to the tribe.

Two months had passed since that day. Suddenly Cassandra wanted to return to that little clearing. Being there wouldn't bring Adam back, but Cassandra's need to walk where he had walked was strong. Hurriedly she scribbled a note to Jodi on a pad of paper, and slipped out the door.

Once on the trail Cassandra relaxed, forgetting for the moment that it was never wise to venture out alone even a short distance into the jungle. It looked innocent enough, this canopy of green that shielded her from the heat of the sun; nevertheless, there were hidden dangers there. Cassandra paused as a snake slithered across the path. This one was harmless enough, she knew, but there were others whose venom could take a life.

Despite the hazards, Cassandra had never been frightened in her jungle home. Its inhabitants were more predictable than many she had met in civilization. The rules were different, but the game of survival was still much the same. Adam knew the rules of both worlds, and Cassandra felt more confident with each passing hour that God would bring him through. If the rebels hadn't captured him, and all indications were that they had not, he and his group may have found shelter with a neighboring tribe. He could just be waiting until the danger passed before returning to base, Cassandra had to believe that.

Continuing on, Cassandra wondered how she'd be able to find the path again. She remembered the lovely spot in the clearing, but she'd been too upset that day to notice how long they'd walked before reaching it. Jungle growth was rapid, with even familiar areas changing if not kept in constant use. Cassandra doubted that anyone would have ventured that way in the past two months.

The crackling sound of a dried twig breaking beneath her foot startled both Cassandra and a family of monkeys that had been peering at her from behind the low branches of a tree. Their high-pitched screeches as they scurried to greater heights added to the chorus of birds and the loud, "tokay, tokay" of a nearby gecko lizard.

Puddles of moisture still remained from the storm two nights before, but there was little other evidence. Circling a low area, Cassandra pushed aside the floppy leaf of a banana tree, avoiding the sticky sap that clung to the stalk's base. A yellow cluster of ripened fruit strained against the dying plant, new shoots already growing up to replace the old. Carefully she skirted a group of low-lying wild orchids, not wanting to crush the delicate lavender blooms.

A few feet past a downed coconut palm Cassandra thought she noticed a break in the vegetation. Quickening her steps, she felt confident that she had found the path; if not, she would soon be forced to turn back or Jodi would be sending the whole village out to look for her.

Cassandra's body ached for her afternoon nap as she paused at the mouth of the trail. The late nights spent worrying about Adam had tired her more than she realized. Though Cassandra's health was rapidly improving, she still had to be cautious not to over-exert herself. The morning spent cleaning and the afternoon's walk was the most exercise she'd had since returning from the hospital, and she was beginning to feel the effects of fatigue.

From her vantage point, Cassandra could almost see her destination. Thankfully, it was still recognizable, though a tangle of vines had twisted through the area and several large branches had broken off the trees during the recent storm. With a heavy sigh she began the short trek, wishing that she'd thought to wear better shoes; her thick rubber thongs were a far cry from the recommended hiking gear.

Entering the clearing, Cassandra spotted a fallen log. She sank down upon it gratefully, using the short reprieve to dislodge a twig from her sandal as she had that day with Adam. The scent of jasmine was stronger than ever—no doubt intensified by the tropical storm, while the lovely orchids, growing in even greater profusion, still trailed from the trees above. Cassandra could almost see Adam sitting on the stump opposite her, his eyes narrowing as he'd pondered the change in her mood. She'd cried in his arms that day, but for all the wrong reasons. Cassandra only wished that she could now be in Adam's arms again, this time shedding tears of joy for his return.

The sound of distant voices filtered through the chatter of the wild, Cassandra only vaguely registering the fact that she was no longer alone. Rebels scouting the area was always a possibility, but as none had been reported, Cassandra dismissed the unwanted intrusion as more likely some of the tribesmen returning from their day's activities.

It was time to be getting back. Jodi would be

worried. Glancing around once more, Cassandra sighed and left the clearing.

The voices became clearer as Cassandra neared the main trail. Pausing, she listened. The smooth tonal quality was unlike the tribal language, or even Cebuan—it sounded decidedly like English! Words were not yet distinguishable, but Cassandra felt certain that the conversation she was overhearing was between an Australian and a woman—Jonathan and Triana?

Forgetting everything, Cassandra rushed toward the trail, eager to question them about Adam. Surely, she surmised, if they'd come to the village to see her, there must be news. Good or bad, she had to know.

Breathlessly Cassandra crashed through the tangled underbrush, heedless of the scratches on her bare legs. "Jonathan! . . . Triana! . . ." Cassandra heard, rather than saw them pass the place where the two trails crossed.

Catching her shoe on a fallen branch, she was forced to stop. "Wait! . . . Please wait!" Frantically she hopped back the few feet to where her sandal was lodged. "Not now," she moaned, tugging at the solidly wedged object and succeeding only in breaking off the piece that secured it to her foot.

"Cassandra. . . ."

Someone was calling her name. She struggled to her feet, the broken sandal forgotten as Cassandra hobbled toward the voice. "Over here!" she cried. "I'm over here!"

The first sight of him was like heaven! Adam flew to her arms, gathering Cassandra to him and raining kisses on each eyelid and down the side of her face before settling his lips hungrily upon hers.

"Cassandra . . . Cassandra, my love," he murmured against her mouth, covering her lips with his own once more. Oblivious to all else, Cassandra took no notice of the two figures walking up behind Adam.

Hand in hand, Jonathan and Triana smiled their approval before turning back down the trail.

Caught up in a kaleidoscope of emotions, Cassandra returned Adam's embrace. "Adam . . . Adam, I was so afraid for you! I was afraid I might never see you again!"

"Hush . . . it's all over now." Adam held Cassandra as if he would never let her go. "Did you doubt I'd come back for you?" he questioned, trailing light kisses down the slender column of her neck. "It was my thoughts of you that kept me going."

Suddenly and without warning, Adam lifted Cassandra into his arms. Snuggling up to him, she wound her arms around his neck. "Where are you taking me?" Her protest was met with that devilish smile that she knew all too well.

Turning, he headed back toward the clearing. "Patience, my love. We can't talk on this overgrown path," he explained, kissing her once more. " . . . and, I'm not ready to share you with Jonathan, Triana, or even Jodi until we've had a chance to really talk."

"Where are Jonathan and Triana?" Suddenly Cassandra recalled that it had been their voices she had heard. "Do they know we're here?"

"They know, but I doubt if they'll notice if we take a little longer getting to the village. . . . I understand they've been creating their own entertainment lately." Laughing at Cassandra's wide-eyed disbelief, Adam's nod confirmed his words. "Uh huh. Seems my little emergency brought them—closer."

Shifting comfortably, Cassandra kissed the tip of Adam's nose. "Tell me about it," she prompted.

"Jonathan and Triana, or my 'little' emergency?"

A shiver went through her as Cassandra thought of the danger Adam had survived. "The rebels," she answered. "Did they really capture you?"

"No," he assured her, readjusting her weight in his arms. "We just had to play native for a few days. Our hosts had no radio, and it wasn't safe to leave."

"Then you did stay with a tribe."

"Uh huh . . . and it gave me a new appreciation for what you're doing—and for you." They were almost at the clearing now, his eyes darting ahead as he spoke. "I've learned a lot these past few days."

Silently he traveled the remaining thirty yards or so, lowering Cassandra gently onto the fallen log. "I'm not saying I've learned all I need to know," he cautioned, raking a hand through his graying hair before slipping into the space beside her. "But I'll never be the man I was before meeting you."

Taking her hand in his, he played absently with the ring finger of her left hand. "I've learned that no matter how much distance I put between us, you'll always be there—a part of me."

The difference in Adam was clearly evident, and Cassandra closed her eyes and offered a silent prayer of thanks even as she leaned against his broad shoulder. She felt warm and safe with Adam so close beside her.

"I was so frightened when I learned you were missing," she confessed, snuggling even closer as he slipped his arm around her and held her tight against him. "But I know now that it was worth it." All that Cassandra had hoped for was coming true and she could hardly contain the joy that was welling up inside her. "God used that experience to bring you home to Him, and then He brought you home to me."

The arm around Cassandra's shoulder slackened at her words. "He brought me home to you. I truly believe that . . . but, my darling, I'm still on the road to coming fully home to Him." A flicker of doubt played across Adam's features, the bright light in his eyes dimming. "I need you, Cassandra. Do you

170

understand? I need you. And I love you—oh, how I love you!''

"And I love you," Cassandra whispered dejectedly, realizing that Adam was pleading for her to meet him halfway on a road with an uncertain end. It was a reasonable request, a compromise she knew many would make. Adam truly was seeking God's direction in a way that he hadn't in years. For that, she was grateful, but was it enough?

"I'm training Jonathan to take over my job." Removing his arm from Cassandra's shoulder, he leaned forward, clasping his hands together as she stared out at the clearing. "I'll be taking a post in Manila. . . ."

Adam—leaving Mindanao? Cassandra's mind raced for a way to make everything right. They needed time. In time it would all work out.

Turning toward her, Adam traced the contours of her face with his forefinger. "I know that what I have to offer isn't perfect, but I love you too much to make promises I'm not yet sure I can keep." Gathering her into his arms, Adam slowly inched his mouth down to hers, the warmth of his breath fanning across her cheeks. "I'm a proud man Cassandra, and I'll only ask you this once . . . Will you marry me?"

CHAPTER 14

DURING THE PAST THREE DAYS the heat had been more oppressive than usual. Cassandra only picked at the lunch she'd helped Jodi to prepare. No one could eat when it was this hot, she reasoned. Setting the fork down, she took a long sip of the cooling liquid before her, trying to avoid the scrutiny of the room's other two occupants.

"I really am better," she asserted, finding it difficult to convince either one of them. "I'm a little tired today, but a good night's sleep will fix that."

"Or a visit from Adam Ralston?" Kindly brown eyes scanned Cassandra's face, a negative shake of his grayed head telling her that he wasn't deceived. "I've known you all your life, Cassie. You're as dear as a daughter to me, and you can't tell me you're well when you're not, or that you're over Adam Ralston when the pain you're feeling is reaching out and touching me, too." Covering Cassandra's hand with his own, George Sanders smiled his understanding. "I think the mission's recommendation that you go home for a while might be a solution to both your problems."

The furlough might give her time to regain her health, but Cassandra knew that a broken heart couldn't be mended so easily. Saying no to Adam that day in the clearing had been the hardest decision of her life. Cassandra knew she'd done the right thing; God had given her His peace. And though the hurt wasn't yet healed, she no longer felt anxious about the situation.

Jonathan Sloan had been the only Pacific Lumber employee to venture down the trail in recent weeks. Once Jonathan had even brought Triana, and Cassandra had found herself almost as pleased as the two of them with the new relationship that had developed. Their own happiness seemed to have sparked an interest in the 'happy ever aftering' of others, often causing Cassandra to wonder about the true nature of the frequent visits. She couldn't bring herself to ask about Adam, but they'd managed to keep her well informed.

A sudden knock at the door caught Cassandra off guard, though neither Jodi nor George appeared surprised by the intrusion.

"That will be Adam," George Sanders informed her smoothly, rising to do the honors as if he were the official host.

"Adam!" Cassandra's voice was a stunned whisper, her riotous thoughts playing ping-pong within the confines of her head. Why was he here? What would she say? Why hadn't she been warned?

"Come in," George invited, gesturing toward an empty place at the table. "We're just finishing lunch. Would you care for anything? Something cool to drink perhaps?"

Slowly Cassandra dared to raise her eyes to meet

174

those of the man she loved. Adam's steady gaze never left hers as he pulled out a chair next to hers.

"Fine," Adam answered absently.

Nervously Cassandra licked her lips, biting down on the lower one as she fought to think of something to say. She wanted to reach out and touch Adam—to be sure he wasn't a figment of her imagination. Her appetite suddenly failing, she pushed her plate aside, ignoring Jodi's disapproving frown.

"You barely touched your food," Adam observed with a quirk at the corner of his mouth. "You'll never gain weight that way."

"I'm . . ." Cassandra squeaked, clearing her tightly restricted throat and swallowing hard. "I'm . . ." she repeated in a still strained voice, ". . . not very hungry right now."

Adam took a sip of the fruity drink, studying Cassandra over the rim of his glass, his expression one of concern.

Noisily shifting his position, George broke the awkward silence, "So, are you all set to go?" he asked of Adam. "Did you manage to get the flight you wanted?"

What flight? Cassandra wondered. Didn't the company plane usually transport the employees and their belongings? Adam was only going as far as Manila, wasn't he? Triana and Jonathan had said nothing more than the fact that Adam would be leaving the area in another three or four weeks. A great deal could happen in that length of time . . . but Cassandra had left it all with the Lord. She gave herself a mental shake.

A warning look passed between Adam and George, causing Cassandra to puzzle even more. There was a strange aura of conspiracy between the two of them. Observing the smile on Jodi's face, she wondered at her involvement as well.

"Yes, the reservation is confirmed, but I still have a couple of details to work out . . . I hope to conclude that part of the arrangements today."

They seemed so pleased with themselves—so smug, Cassandra decided. She was dying to know what they were all obviously keeping from her. She felt like a kid who hadn't been invited to play the game—only it wasn't a game.

"Okay . . . ," Cassandra finally demanded, her tone matching the glint in her eyes. "What's going on here?"

Jodi was the first to crack, her slow giggle rising until she could contain it no longer.

"Did I ever tell you you're adorable when you're mad?" Adam grinned.

"I'm not mad!" Cassandra screamed above the laughter of her friends. Pushing back slightly, she planted her elbows squarely on the table, joining her two hands in a fist. "But I'm going to be if someone doesn't tell me what's going on."

For a full minute they fought for control, Cassandra watching as even George had to bring a handkerchief out to wipe away the tears. "Well," she sighed, once a modicum of order had been restored. "Is someone going to put me out of my misery?"

"Go on, Dr. Ralston," George laughed. "Put the poor girl out of her misery."

"Come, Cassandra," Adam prompted, the expression in his eyes taking the last of the fire from hers. "George and I have had a lot of time to talk these last weeks when I've been in Butuan . . . I think it's time we had ours."

As if in a dream, Cassandra allowed Adam to lead her out the door and down to the trail that had always provided the physical link between them. As she walked beside him, she felt a strange new bond that transcended any they had shared before. The arm that

176

Adam had draped casually across Cassandra's shoulders tightened, and she snuggled against him the way she'd been wanting to ever since he'd entered her door.

The familiar jungle seemed to welcome them as they strolled silently. There were so many questions Cassandra needed to ask, but none that couldn't wait until they'd reached the clearing where she felt confident Adam was taking her. She was both eager and frightened to hear what Adam had to say. If he again declared his love, Cassandra wasn't certain she'd be able to refuse him a second time. She only hoped that the change she'd sensed in him was real, not merely the product of her intense desire.

"Curious?" Adam smiled, catching her expression.

"Uh huh," Cassandra admitted openly. "More than curious . . . suspicious!"

Removing his arm from around her shoulders, Adam extended his hand and Cassandra complied by placing hers inside. "We'll talk in the clearing." Glancing down at Cassandra's feet, Adam shook his head. "Won't you ever learn not to wear sandals in the jungle?"

"I usually wear sneakers or hiking boots, but you didn't say where we were going. Besides, you never *ask*, Adam, you just *order*!"

"Maybe I should have ordered you to marry me!" Adam exclaimed, before scooping her up into his arms. "It could have saved me a lot of trouble."

"Put me down, Adam Ralston!" Cassandra complained, ignoring his comment. "I *can* walk!"

"Not very well," he argued, striding forward with Cassandra in his arms.

Cassandra knew better than to struggle. Locking her arms around his neck, she decided to give in, determined that she would make the return trip on her own two feet—sandals or not!

It wasn't long until he was gently lowering her onto the now familiar log. Like the reserving of a favorite table in a favorite restaurant, the clearing was waiting for them—the same trees, the same orchids, the same man and woman feeling the same feelings. Swallowing hard, Cassandra tried not to anticipate the outcome of this afternoon. It might be too painful.

Cassandra stiffened as Adam came to sit beside her. She wanted to believe that by some miracle things were really different now, but Cassandra wasn't sure. It was frightening to love someone so much and not be sure that it was right to accept his love in return.

"Relax," Adam admonished, placing his hands on her shoulders and turning her to face him. "I haven't come back into your life to hurt you, Cassandra." The words were spoken softly and the sincerity of his love shone from his eyes.

"Then . . . why have you come back?"

"I had to." Reaching behind her, Adam unfastened the clasp that held Cassandra's hair, reminding her of the day that he'd first brought her to their clearing. "At worst . . . At worst, I've come to say goodbye—" The tight line of Adam's jaw revealed his distress.

"And at best?"

Lifting Cassandra's once-bound tresses, Adam released his gentle grip, watching as the silken strands fell about her shoulders. "I think I'll leave the 'at best' to you."

Rising, Adam ignored Cassandra's stunned expression. Walking over to the tree trunk, his grin widened to the proportions of a Cheshire cat. "George said you wouldn't do it . . . not even when you learn I've given my life back to the Lord and plan to continue my medical mission training."

"You've done *what*?" Cassandra's loud gasp

178

pierced the near silence, multiplying the decibel level of the jungle sounds.

"Well . . . with things as they are in Mindanao, I can't guarantee that when I finish my training, the doors will still be open here. But I feel stronger now than ever about the need for a medical support clinic for the tribal missions."

"You mean it?" Cassandra's eyes shone with the delight of a child on Christmas morning. "You really mean it?"

"I mean it," Adam answered, opening his arms to her and cradling her close.

"I love you!" she announced, hugging him to her.

"Hmmm," Adam sighed, after receiving and returning Cassandra's kisses. "That part didn't take long."

"What part?" Cassandra asked, content only to savor the joy of his nearness.

Twining his fingers through her hair, Adam brought Cassandra's lips down again upon his before releasing her. "I still have one more problem."

"Problem?" Cassandra dismissed, teasing his jawline with a trail of tiny kisses. "I can't see any problems."

"Now behave," Adam laughed. "I need your help with a solution."

"Okay," she pouted, sitting up poker-straight. "Is this what you want?"

"Not exactly," Adam laughed, planting a kiss on her pursed lips. "I have it from a reliable source that most missions prefer married couples on the field. I tend to agree with that policy . . . don't you?"

"Absolutely!"

"Hmm . . . you do?" Lifting Cassandra's chin, Adam rained soft butterfly kisses on her lips. "I leave in three weeks. . . . Got anyone in mind?"

"I might," she teased, enjoying Adam's playful

mood. "There's a stubborn . . . self-willed . . ." With each word Cassandra traced tiny circles around his mouth with her finger. ". . . lady missionary. I know her quite well."

"And why should I choose her? Could it be possible that she needs her own private physician?"

"You might say that. You might even say it's your Christian duty to marry her."

"Really?" Adam pulled away. "Seems that I proposed to someone of that description once—but she turned me down."

"Oh, if you asked her again, I'm sure she wouldn't refuse," Cassandra insisted, aching to hear those words that would cement their vows of love.

To Cassandra's surprise, Adam began to ease her from his lap. "A man's ego is awfully fragile . . . I might not want to chance being turned down again."

It took several moments before it registered with Cassandra that no proposal had been made. Slowly, from the recesses of her memory, she recalled that Adam had said he would issue only one offer of marriage. Surely he didn't intend to abide by those hastily spoken words. Or did he?

"You don't expect *me* . . ."

The crooked grin on his face assured her he had every intention of holding to his declaration.

"You *do* !" Cassandra gasped, at a loss as to what to do next.

Casually, Adam stood, brushed out the creases in his pants, and without even a backward glance took several steps toward the path that led to the main trail. "Well . . . I guess this is goodbye."

"Adam!" Rushing forward, Cassandra placed a restraining hand on his arm. "Don't go. Please."

"Was there something you wanted to ask me?" Adam grinned mischievously.

"No. I guess not," she stated stubbornly, releasing his arm.

"You sure about that?" he tempted, gathering her into his arms and slowly, very slowly lowering his lips to within an inch of hers.

"Adam, I can't! I just can't!" she protested, before his mouth came down once more, catching her up in the passion of his embrace.

In his arms she felt complete. In his arms anywhere would be Eden for her. Together they could make their own paradise—at times, less than perfect perhaps, but a paradise that would be based on the love of their God and their love for each other.

Breathlessly Cassandra considered their future. "Okay," she conceded finally, a hint of a smile tugging at her lower lip. " . . . But if you ever tell anyone, Adam Ralston. . . ."

Planting a quick kiss on the bridge of Cassandra's nose, Adam chuckled at her threat, his expression becoming ever more smug as he anticipated her proposal. "Go on," he prompted, "I'm waiting."

Casting her eyes shyly downward, Cassandra slowly lifted them to Adam and whispered, "Will you marry me?"

Closing his eyes, Adam inhaled sharply. For a panicky second Cassandra feared that he was going to refuse her.

"Adam? . . . Did you hear me?"

In a flash his smile returned. Grabbing her around the waist, he caught her to him joyously.

"I thought you'd never ask," he laughed, withdrawing a folder from his pocket and handing it to Cassandra. At her puzzled expression, he explained, "They're airline tickets made out to Mr. and Mrs. Adam Ralston."

Wide-eyed, Cassandra stared at the papers. "You

knew I'd do it, didn't you! Ohhh, you insufferable, egotistical . . ."

". . . arrogant loggerman!" he finished, capturing the fists that were pummeling his chest. "I love you, Cassandra, my love. And I'd be honored to have you as my wife!"

MEET THE AUTHOR

While attending Bible college in her native Miami, Florida, BARBARA BENNETT met her husband of twelve years. Despite six company relocations, the Bennetts have been actively involved in a wide range of ministries, ranging from the establishment of outreach youth work to the co-founding of a Hebrew-Christian church. In addition, they are the parents of two young daughters and currently reside in Houston, Texas.

Barbara has traveled to sixteen foreign countries and has lived in or visited over half of the United States. Her love of travel and her fascination with world cultures are reflected in her writing. FOREVER EDEN is her first published novel.

A Letter To Our Readers

Dear Reader:

Pioneering is an exhilarating experience, filled with opportunities for exploring new frontiers. The Zondervan Corporation is proud to be the first major publisher to launch a series of inspirational romances designed to inspire and uplift as well as to provide wholesome entertainment. In order that we might better contribute to your reading enjoyment, we would appreciate your taking a few minutes to respond to the following questions and return to:

> Anne Severance, Editor
> Zondervan Publishing House
> 1415 Lake Drive
> Grand Rapids, Michigan   49506

1. Did you enjoy reading FOREVER EDEN?

    ☐ Very much. I would like to see more books by this author!
    ☐ Moderately.
    ☐ I would have enjoyed it more if _____

2. Where did you purchase this book? _____

3. What influenced your decision to purchase this book?

    ☐ Cover   ☐ Back cover copy
    ☐ Title   ☐ Friends
    ☐ Publicity   ☐ Other _____

4. Please rate the following elements from 1 (poor) to 10 (superior).

☐ Heroine   ☐ Plot
☐ Hero   ☐ Inspirational theme
☐ Setting   ☐ Secondary characters

5. Which settings would you like to see in future Serenade/Saga Books?

_____   _____

_____   _____

6. What are some inspirational themes you would like to see treated in future books?

_____   _____

_____   _____

7. Would you be interested in reading other Serenade/Serenata or Serenade/Saga Books?

☐ Very interested
☐ Moderately interested
☐ Not interested

8. Please indicate your age range:

☐ Under 18   ☐ 25–34   ☐ 46–55
☐ 18–24   ☐ 35–45   ☐ Over 55

9. Would you be interested in a Serenade book club? If so, please give us your name and address:

Name _____

Occupation _____

Address _____

City _____ State _____ Zip _____

Serenade/Serenata Books are inspirational romances in contemporary settings, designed to bring you a joyful, heart-lifting reading experience.

Other Serenade books available in your local bookstore:

#1 ON WINGS OF LOVE, Elaine L. Schulte
#2 LOVE'S SWEET PROMISE,
      Susan C. Feldhake
#3 FOR LOVE ALONE, Susan C. Feldhake
#4 LOVE'S LATE SPRING, Lydia Heermann
#5 IN COMES LOVE, Mab Graff Hoover
#6 FOUNTAIN OF LOVE, Velma S. Daniels and
      Peggy E. King.
#7 MORNING SONG, Linda Herring
#8 A MOUNTAIN TO STAND STRONG,
      Peggy Darty
#9 LOVE'S PERFECT IMAGE, Judy Baer
#10 SMOKY MOUNTAIN SUNRISE,
      Yvonne Lehman
#11 GREENGOLD AUTUMN, Donna F. Crow
#12 IRRESISTIBLE LOVE, Elaine Anne McAvoy
#13 ETERNAL FLAME, Lurlene McDaniel

Watch for forthcoming books in both the contemporary and historical series coming soon to your local book store:

#16 CALL OF THE DOVE, Madge Harrah
      (Serenata)
#15 SPEAK SOFTLY, LOVE, Kathleen Yapp
      (Saga)
#16 FROM THIS DAY FORWARD, Kathleen Karr
      (Saga)